I moved closer, not making a sound. The wind drifted through the forest, making more noise than I did. Alleen saw me. Her eyes widened a little but she gave no other sign.

The man grunted out, "Kill you, bitch. You made me less than a man. Never have children. No sons. Kill." He was in stark pain. I took care of that the instant he turned to find a more comfortable position before he killed the woman.

My stiletto flashed in the sunlight filtering through the trees. The guerrilla stiffened and fell to one side. The blade had entered between the second and third vertebrae at the base of his neck. He twitched like a beheaded snake, then ceased moving altogether.

I cleaned Wilhelmina, then checked Alleen. She looked as if she was in shock. With all she had had to endure, it was no wonder.

We left. Alleen needed some serious psychiatric care and I couldn't give it to her. All I could do was nursemaid her until we got back to civilization.

And that wouldn't be until after I eliminated Doctor DNA.

NICK CARTER IS IT!

"Nick Carter out-Bonds James Bond."
—*Buffalo Evening News*

"Nick Carter is America's #1 espionage agent."
—*Variety*

"Nick Carter is razor-sharp suspense."
—*King Features*

"Nick Carter is extraordinarily big."
—*Bestsellers*

"Nick Carter has attracted an army of addicted readers . . . the books are fast, have plenty of action and just the right degree of sex . . . Nick Carter is the American James Bond, suave, sophisticated, a killer with both the ladies and the enemy."

–*The New York Times*

FROM THE NICK CARTER KILLMASTER SERIES

A Killmaster Spy Chiller

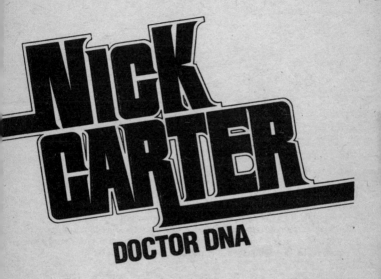

NICK CARTER

DOCTOR DNA

ACE CHARTER BOOKS, NEW YORK

An Ace Charter Original

Published by arrangement with The Condé Nast Publications, Inc.

ISBN: 0-441-15676-2

First Ace Charter Printing: November 1982
Published simultaneously in Canada

Manufactured in the United States of America
Ace Books, 200 Madison Avenue, New York, New York 10016

Dedicated to the men of the
Secret Services of the
United States of America

DOCTOR DNA

CHAPTER ONE

It was like a blow to my gut. I held down my rising gorge and tried to go with the flow, to get my sea legs. It proved virtually impossible. I'd been too used to air travel, the smooth flight of subsonic commercial jetliners and the buffeting of supersonic military jets to appreciate the rocking of the Atlantic Ocean.

The storm was small in comparison to another we'd weathered less than two days prior. The radioman delighted in telling me of another storm that would hit us two days out of Walvis Bay, Namibia, going south to Cape Town. I wasn't fooling anyone into believing I was an experienced seaman. The sight of my green face and the sound of my churning belly would put anything I said otherwise to the lie.

I hated this charade, yet part of my job required it. I was on an undercover assignment. I'm Nick Carter, Killmaster and agent N3 for the super-secret organization AXE.

Every time the ship, badly misnamed *The Easy Ride*,

rolled in the storm wracking the ocean, another muscle tensed inside me. I forced myself to relax. Seasickness is as much a matter of mental discomfort as it is physical. I wished I had one of those fancy new gadgets that sticks behind the ear like a bandage and slowly releases anti-motion sickness medicine through the skin. I had nothing like that. Clinging to the sides of my bunk, I closed my eyes and forced myself through mental-calming exercises I'd learned a long time ago.

It helped. Enough.

"Hey, Carter," called out one of my fellow seamen. "Wanna bite of this? It's boa constrictor meat. Got it when we put into port at Monrovia." Achmed ben-Gorra bit down on a piece of the too-white meat, gripped it firmly with his teeth and expertly slashed it off with a flick of his razor-sharp knife. He made a big production of gnawing and enjoying.

"Ate already," I said. "Years ago. And that was still too soon." The black giant of a man laughed at my discomfort and went back to his meal.

While my cover as able-bodied seaman fooled no one aboard *The Easy Ride*, it didn't matter. Most of them weren't seamen; they were refugees. What they ran from encompassed the entire spectrum of worldly problems. Some were murderers fleeing justice and the outraged families of their victims; some fancied themselves world travelers; still others were unable to find any other job. I'd boarded in Rabat, Morocco, with two others. None of us was a trained seaman. I'd hoped to get a job as purser or navigator trainee. No such luck on a decrepit scow like this.

I bent my back with the rest, loading and unloading. As it turned out, this worked to my benefit. It put me down on the docks where I could watch the activity around me.

Our brief layover in Monrovia was necessary because *The Easy Ride* was registered in Liberia for tax reasons. The owners lived in France and the ship carried any cargo it could find that needed freighting—whether that cargo was legal or not. David Hawk, my boss at AXE, hadn't sent me to Africa to stop gun-runners, though. AXE deals only with the highest-level international intrigues.

High-level intrigue, low-level position. It seemed to go with the territory.

I'd been assigned to establish a cover—seaman—on a coast-hugging ship and make my way slowly down to South Africa. The Union of South Africa had never been a particularly good ally of the United States and, for sound diplomatic reasons, we didn't want it to appear to the world that we approved of South Africa's internal racial policies. There was no getting around the fact, however, that we needed the raw materials this country had to offer. "Strategic metals" was the current buzzword for the cobalt needed for jet engine turbines, manganese for lightweight alloys, and the diamonds and gold and all the rest that came up from underground in South Africa. We needed these for national security. South Africa was willing to sell, in exchange for products they couldn't provide for themselves—like oil.

The trading went on in an almost clandestine fashion, everyone washing their hands afterward.

The trading went on, that is, until the government ministers in the South African cabinet began dying. A bit of digging unearthed the answer to the cessation of normal shipping. Someone had instituted one of the most elaborate extortion rackets ever conceived in modern times. The ministers doing the dying had refused to buckle under to the unknown extortionist's demands.

They died horribly—and of natural causes.

Natural causes covers a variety of ugly ways of checking out. Two ministers had cashed in via sleeping sickness. One had died from lhassa fever, one of the most virulent diseases on the face of the earth. Still another had contracted green monkey fever, so rare it took a team of specialists over a week of intensive autopsy to identify it. All had died precisely when the extortionist had said they would.

Nothing causes a bureaucrat more fear than someone else being right in a prediction. These deaths were documented.

And the extortion had begun in full force less than a week later, other ministers slowing shipments to the U.S., still others demanding that we renegotiate contracts in good standing for years. They were scared and caved in to the unidentified terrorist's every demand.

AXE and the United States wouldn't stand for this cessation of vital shipments. Nor would we stand for someone meddling in the internal affairs of another country in this manner. Worst of all, the powers-that-be in Washington had no idea how the extortion was being pulled off. The best medical doctors flatly denied the possibility of such specific targeting for a disease. They claimed it amounted to nothing more than chance. Even the bright boys in the Nuclear-Biological-Chemical warfare unit at Fort Detrick, Maryland, scratched their heads and said it wasn't possible to deliver any NBC weapon with such precision.

AXE had evidence it happened four times in the span of a month. Some genius had found a new way to kill and had started using it.

"Hey, man," came the cry from across the room. "Got good news for you, man."

"You cut your own tongue out with that knife," I said. My stomach had settled and I felt more human now. I'd live.

"No, man, better'n that. We make Walvis Bay by dawn. You will have dirt under your feet again."

"Great," I said. "That also means we got to unload this barge."

"What's a little work, man?" Achmed laughed, his teeth white in the jet blackness of his face. I peered at him, trying to figure him out. He was the only one of the crew that tried to make friends with me. I couldn't tell if it was just his way or if there were ulterior motives.

Sometimes, being a spy generates a bit of paranoia.

"Wake me when we hit port," I said, rolling over. I lay awake for long minutes, my spine tingling as if waiting for that huge, razor-edged knife to slash vital nerves. When it didn't come, I went to sleep.

*   *   *

Every muscle in my body ached. Being a stevedore is about the hardest work I've ever done. I cursed Hawk under my breath. He'd said there wouldn't be any problem getting a nice, cozy job up on the bridge. I know enough to navigate a ship, can keep records with the best purser afloat, and could probably captain this scow better than Captain Svensen on his best day. Svensen spent his time drunk in his cabin. The first officer, a taciturn Pole, ran *The Easy Ride* as if it were his own command—which, in a way, it was. Captain or first officer, the title didn't matter. When Lt. Polochek gave an order, everyone obeyed.

Walvis Bay, Namibia, was neither better nor worse than any of the other ports along Africa's west coast. The docking area needed repair and the people who weren't half-starved appeared less than interested in working. Even though I'd done my homework for this assignment, it still surprised me when I heard more Afrikaans being spoken in port than any other language. Namibia was, in theory, a free country. In practice the Union of South Africa controlled it totally and the Union, as its citizens referred to it, had been settled by tough Dutch farmers in the seventeenth century. The Dutch-Afrikaans and German languages are close enough so that I managed to overhear and understand a great deal.

But none of it pertained to my mission. I really didn't care if the Democratic Turnhalle Alliance represented the working people or not. I needed information on a man able to induce hideous diseases seemingly by remote control.

I did my job, I listened to the bitching about the DTA, and I fell back into my bunk that night as *The Easy Ride* put to sea. All in a day's work for a spy.

Tossing and turning, I felt every lump in the hard pad under me. The ocean was like glass this night, silky smooth and seductively peaceful. It wasn't the motion of the ship, then, that brought me fully awake.

Over the years, I've cultivated a sixth sense. People in other professions have different varieties of it. Athletes anticipate the starting gun by fractions of a second—the fractions of a second needed to win. High steel workers know when to drop down on hands and knees and crawl seventy stories above the cold, hard pavement. I know when danger is nearby.

Appearing to do nothing more than roll over, I tucked the pillow firmly under my head. In the same motion, I found my trusty Luger, Wilhelmina. Opening my eyes slowly, I studied the cramped quarters. Achmed had pulled the graveyard shift tonight. So had the three others sharing our dingy metal box of a compartment. One of them might have decided to deadhead a bit and grab a little sleep even though he was supposed to be on watch.

Maybe. I doubted it. The shadow I spotted at the far side of the compartment moved too slowly, too deliberately. If it had been one of the crew coming in, they wouldn't have given so much as a whisker from Neptune's beard whether they woke me or not. My nocturnal visitor moved cautiously and quietly.

I tensed, my finger tightening just enough to convince me that a 9mm Parabellum round would be on its way with only the slightest movement on my part. I didn't want to kill the man; I wanted him alive. If he came in here like a thief, that meant he either was a thief—or he was after me. If the latter, my cover was already compromised and I provided a handy, highly visible target for the extortionist running the South African government by fear.

If my cover had been blown, it also meant I had a chance to get real information from my attacker.

A curious humming sound filled the metal-walled room. At first I thought it was an old-time tube radio warming up but the subharmonics were wrong for that. An electrical gadget of some sort had been turned on. That was all I knew. I quickly thought about jumping out of bed; I feared the device might be a metal detector able to pinpoint Wilhelmina or my stiletto, Hugo. I decided to wait and see what happened.

Another buzzing noise came, more muted than the first, more natural. It circled above my head. I eyed it suspiciously. When I recognized it as another of the damned flying insects that blight all of Africa, a curious mixture of relief and alarm filled me.

In port we were bedeviled by bugs. At sea, the only pests we contended with were rats and insects living off the cargo, if we carried produce. What we had in the hold now was inorganic. Still, an insect shouldn't have inspired the fear in me this one did, whether or not we had a hold filled with fruits and vegetables.

My sixth sense told me to act.

In a smooth, flowing motion, I abandoned my Luger, scooped up a packet of mosquito netting from under my bunk and cast it like a cowboy throwing a lariat. The light nylon netting descended and neatly captured the offending insect in midair. The weight of the net held the bug firmly pinned to my bunk.

"Damn," came the single curse from my visitor. The electronic hum vanished as the man spun and darted through the hatchway. I followed, my bare feet making slapping noises against the cold metal deck.

Bursting through the hatch leading to open air, I paused and glanced both left and right. I saw no one. The night breeze touched my skin, warm and humid, almost a lover's caress. The bright moon dangling above the horizon was the sort that inspires mediocre poets to rhyme with June and spoon. Salt and paint and grease tainted the otherwise clean air and gave no clue to my intruder's whereabouts. But the sound of harsh panting gave him away.

I moved silently toward the stern of the ship. Creaking and whistling noises from the engines below occasionally hid the panicked breathing, but I had him located now. He'd hidden behind one of the lifeboats. The boat itself was for display purposes only. I'd checked it out on first boarding *The Easy Ride*. The lifeboat's bottom sported more holes than a slice of Swiss cheese. My quarry hid behind that lifeboat now, maybe peering through one of the holes at me.

Even though I wore a pair of shorts, I felt totally naked.

Both Wilhelmina and Hugo remained in my bunk. Only my tiny gas bomb Pierre rode in his usual place, a skinlike pouch high on the inside of my right thigh. But in the open, with a breeze blowing, Pierre's deadly effects would be minimal. I had to depend on my own wits to stay alive.

I wasn't worried.

My legs bent and instant calculation flashed through my mind. Like a bolt of lightning, I launched myself at precisely the right instant. My arms found spindly legs. I tightened my grip and the man fell headlong to the metal deck as he foolishly tried to run.

A large black leather bag, almost like a photographer's camera case, went bounding from his grip, hit the railing and vanished into the Atlantic. I didn't stop to ask him what he'd lost. I had my hands full of kicking legs. A lucky shot caught me right on the chin. Stars wheeled around to join the gibbous moon. By the time I regained my senses, my quarry had fled again.

But he didn't get far. I caught him in less than three long paces.

I spun him around and got a good look at him. Black. Native. Maybe Bantu or Xhosa. He was better fed than most I'd seen so far, but he still had a long way to go before even an ounce of fat showed on his body. Spindly legs and matchstick arms flailed wildly. He wasn't much of a fighter.

I shoved him against the rail, waited for him to rebound, then chose a spot on the tip of his chin and let fly a short jab. The crunch sounded from one end of the ship to the other. My would-be attacker fell without a single outcry.

"What's goin' on?" came a thick voice. "Who's back there messin' round?"

"Just me, Achmed," I called out, recognizing the voice. "Go back to your drinking. I . . . I just had to upchuck."

"Man, this sea's smoother'n a French whore's tit. What you doin' back there?"

I didn't want Achmed investigating. Turning to my captive, I rolled him onto his belly, shook him partially awake and then stuck my finger down his throat. Weak gagging noises were all I could get. Whenever he'd eaten last, all the food had been digested and had run into his intestines. Still, the vomiting sounds kept Achmed at bay.

"Man, you got the weakest stomach of any fucker I ever seen." The giant black didn't pursue my *mal de mer* any further.

Wiping off my hand on my captive's tattered cotton shirt, I pulled him to a sitting position. I pressed my knuckles into the sides of his throat, found the tiny buttons of muscle protecting the carotid arteries and rolled them away. The slightest pressure now would cut off blood to the brain. I could knock out my unwanted guest in seconds.

"Listen carefully," I told him in a low voice. "I want answers. If I don't get them, this is going to happen." I tightened up. When his eyes began to bug out, I loosened up on the pressure. Waiting for the blood to course through his neck again and clear his brain, I added, "That's what you get if you try to escape. Got it?"

He nodded.

"So who sent you?"

"Nobody, mister. Honest." I tensed my muscles but didn't apply any pressure. The effect was the same. "Honest, I don't know his name."

"Who are you?"

"Just nuthin'."

"What tribe?"

"Bantu." I'd been right on that score. Give me a gold star for good research.

"You came aboard ship at Walvis Bay." He nodded. "To kill me." I didn't make that a question. It came out as a flat statement. The way his eyes widened told me it was the truth. "Now for the hard part. How were you supposed to do it? What was that gadget you had with you?"

"I dunno!"

I choked him out. My knuckles cut into his thin neck until the arteries shut down. I held it for about four seconds, then released my grip. I didn't want to kill him, just show him he had more to fear from me than his nameless boss back in Namibia. Shaking him hard brought his large eyes open again.

"Don't lie. What was the bag you carried aboard?"

"He gave it to me. He tell me to turn the dials this way'n that. He say it was all I had to do to make the money." Curiosity forced me to ask how much this hit had cost. I've had hit men paid upward of half a million to remove me. I let out a low sigh of resignation when he told me, "Five dollar. He pay me five dollar."

I would have been dead meat for a lousy five bucks.

"You keep saying 'he.' Who is this 'he' that gave you the five dollars to kill me?" I tensed enough to show him I meant business.

"He called Doctor DNA."

I almost laughed and called him a liar, then I stopped. This wasn't the sort of lie I'd expect from an obviously starved, uneducated man. The way he said it also told me that he feared this Doctor DNA more than he did me; yet I was the one with a death grip on his scrawny throat.

"The insect," I said, my mind racing. "What about it?"

"I . . . I turn it loose from the bag. Then I spin the knobs and point the stick. Thass all I know, honest, man!"

What he said made little sense, but getting more information from him seemed unlikely. Unfortunately, as I considered all this, the man felt my grip weaken appreciably. He surged up with surprising strength and jerked free. Instinct and training can sometimes work against me. Without thinking, I kicked a leg out from under him and swung another short jab to his midsection. I felt ribs crack. The man gasped, spit pink foam, and collapsed, his eyes rolling up.

I'd broken a rib and punctured his lung. The man's physical condition was poor to start with; he died within a minute, drowning in his own blood. I hadn't meant to kill him, but it had happened. Even though he'd been sent to permanently remove me from the game, I felt some remorse for him. He wasn't one of the usual players, one of the superbly trained, magnificently armed barracudas swimming in the world of international intrigue. He was a pathetic, hungry man from a dusty inland village trying to earn a lousy five dollars, nothing more. I pushed him over the side. His body hit the ocean waters twenty feet below with only the smallest of splashes.

Achmed called out, "You done pukin' your guts out yet, Carter? For a man who don't eat much, you sure do lose a lot."

"I'm okay, Achmed," I called out. I returned to my hard bunk and carefully transferred the insect still trapped under the netting to a small vial.

I wanted some souvenir of this night's deadly interlude to show to Hawk.

CHAPTER TWO

The Easy Ride swung around the bulge of Africa and headed for Cape Town. The sight made me suck in my breath and hold it for a moment. The beauty of Table Mountain rising up between the shorter Devil's Peak and the Lion's Head was worth every ache in my body. The mountainsides were ablaze with glorious colors from more varieties of wildflower than existed in all the British Isles. It looked as if some drunken artist had dropped his palette and the colors had run down to the sea. Together with the clean, warm breeze sneaking around the Cape of Good Hope from the Indian Ocean and the lighter wind at my back coming off the cold South Atlantic, the miasma from those flowers produced the most heady aroma I'd ever smelled.

"Get your ass movin', man," came Achmed's command. "We be in port in less than twenty minutes."

"Make that an hour," I replied. "Svensen decided to pilot us in this time. All by himself."

13

"Allah be merciful," the man muttered under his breath. Achmed joined me at the rail and peered inland. "It is God's bounty. And it is wasted on those *kaffirs*."

I said nothing. I wasn't about to get embroiled in a political or religious argument with this giant of a man. Christianity made up most of the religion in South Africa—I'd heard it was the fastest growing area of Catholicism in the world. And I knew already how South Africa treated blacks. Achmed, being a black Mohammedan, would be out of place on two different fronts.

"I do not like this port. Even miserable Walvis Bay, it is better. But the ship comes here, so we work, eh, man?"

"We work," I agreed. "How long you been at sea, Achmed?"

"All my life, it seems. No, it *is* all my life. I barely walked when I stowed away on a Greek freighter. Those Greeks are fighters. They do things different from any other crew."

"Such as?"

"They train cats. You ever see a cat fetch like a dog? Roll over and play dead? Sit up and beg? The Greeks they spend hours, days, even years aboard ship. Their officers are afraid they will jump ship in harbor so none ever get shore leave. They are prisoners. And the best damn sailors I ever been with."

"Getting shore leave isn't all that great, at least for you." I lifted my chin and indicated Cape Town. "Not with things the way they are there."

"Apartheid," he said, spitting out the word so that it sounded like he'd said, "Apart-hate."

I glanced out of the corner of my eye at him, wondering if my intuition could be so far wrong. Everything about him spoke of courage and power beyond anyone else in the crew; yet he acted almost docile when confronting the officers. Maybe it was the early training he'd received aboard Greek ships. I didn't know. I just felt there was more to Achmed than met the eye—and that I had nothing to fear from him.

"You jumpin' ship here, man?" he asked suddenly.

I covered, although the question took me by surprise.

"You don't miss much, do you?" I glanced around. Lt. Polochek stood beside the captain on the bridge, his cold, dark eyes watching every movement of his senior officer for miscalculation and mistake. None of the other officers was within earshot. "I doubt I'll be back aboard *The Easy Ride* any time soon."

"Why you runnin', Carter? You don' belong on the sea, but I be damn if I know where you do belong."

I shrugged.

"The usual, I guess. Why are most of the men aboard this garbage scow?"

"You're not runnin' *from* something," Achmed said positively. "Might be you're runnin' *to* something."

"That's a beautiful place to run to, if you're right." I took in the awesome beauty of Cape Town again before the ship started into the garbage-strewn harbor crowded with run-down ships of all descriptions.

"On the outside. Underneath, she be rotted. You see, mark my words."

"I'll remember that, Achmed. Thanks."

His dark eyes bored into mine for a long moment, then he smiled, white teeth seemingly flashing from ear to ear. He slapped me on the shoulder so hard it jolted me.

"We unload. We show them how real seamen work. Then you go live with the maggots inside that beautiful fruit you call Cape Town."

I leaned back against a stuccoed building and smoked a leisurely cigarette. I'd earned it. The ship was unloaded in record time and the captain had told everyone to take an hour break while he found the harbormaster to arrange for the next cargo. Whenever Captain Svensen ran down that new cargo, I'd be gone. But first I wanted to sit, smoke, and listen.

Most of all, I listened.

As in Walvis Bay, Afrikaans dominated the spoken conversations. It didn't take long to figure out the caste system, even if I hadn't known about it before. Blacks were always referred to as "natives." The Cape Coloreds were an intermediate caste, neither black nor accepted as white. They were mixtures of Hottentot, Malay, and British seamen, and more often than not held minor managerial positions.

Nowhere did I see an important post being held by a black.

Hawk had told me that the extortion payments were being demanded in the very strategic metals denied to the United States. Cobalt, tungsten, manganese, and the others are heavy. And, compared to gold and diamonds, they aren't worth very much. A hundred dollars a kilo is the outside price on most of them while gold currently sells worldwide at around sixteen thousand a kilo. Still, an entire boatload of metal amounts to several thousand tons. And the strategic metals would be easier to sell on the world market.

Easier to sell, but more difficult to get out of the country. Even with ministers of transportation and customs looking the other way out of fear, ships had to be used to get the extortion payments out of South Africa. Where did those ships go? Who crewed them? These were tidbits Hawk desperately needed to know.

Even the scuttlebutt along the docks seemed censored, edited, predigested. No one spoke out boldly against the latest government regulation, whatever it might be. No one spoke of the panic running through the government, though most of the men sensed it. Every time a uniformed official walked along the dock, a small stiffening took place and an unnatural silence fell.

I wished I'd been in the Union before, during more normal times. It proved difficult to tell if this behavior was natural or if it came from the fear that the official might be a carrier for any of a half-dozen deadly contagious diseases.

Tossing my cigarette butt into the oily harbor, I stood and made a quick check. Wilhelmina and Hugo rested in their usual places. The Luger fit snugly under my left arm while the stiletto was in a spring-loaded sheath on my right forearm. A slight tensing of the muscles would send the knife out and into my grip for instant defense. Most of my meager belongings remained aboard *The Easy Ride*. I neither needed nor wanted them and didn't want to advertise the fact I was jumping ship.

One thing that I had brought with me was the tiny vial containing the insect captured the night before. Bringing it out, I tapped the side of the bottle and watched the bug go crazy inside, buzzing and thrashing about in a vain attempt to escape through the clear glass.

"What you got there, man?" came a familiar voice. I turned and saw Achmed towering over me. I'm six feet—he topped me by an easy six inches.

"Caught the little devil. Do you know what it is?" I didn't release the bottle from my grip and Achmed didn't make a move to take it. From the disgust on his face, I knew he'd already identified the insect.

"That's one bad bug, man. A tsetse fly. You don't want to be stung by him, no sir. Kill him, Carter. He carries the sleeping sickness."

"I'll hang onto him a little longer," I said, tucking the bottle away safely into a pocket.

"The captain has cargo." Achmed stood, his eyes boring into me again as if he searched my soul.

"Thanks," I said. In his own way he'd told me to split now. Otherwise, I'd be trapped into loading *The Easy Ride* and from then on would be under the supervision of the ship's officers. I held out my hand. For a moment I thought he was going to shake it. He sadly backed away a full pace.

"This is the Union, man. You go to jail if they see you bein' friendly to a black man."

"What about you?" I asked.

He laughed harshly. "They might let me live to stand trial, man. That'd be the worst they could do. Go now."

I went.

And I immediately sensed that someone followed me. At first, I thought it might have been coincidence. There weren't too many ways off a dock. When I reached the end of the pier

and turned toward the Lion's Head, they still followed. I
doubled back and got a good look at them. There were two
men, white, dressed in seamen's clothes, well built and
looking as if they'd been in a lot of dockside fights—and had
won them all.

I cut away sharply, walking up a street perpendicular to the
one I'd been on, then made another right turn and paralleled
my original course. I summoned a cab.

"Down to Cape Point," I told him.

"Long way," came the laconic answer. "You got
money?"

I shoved a British twenty pound note at him. He grinned
and took off. I casually glanced behind and saw another car
following. Three men were inside. The interior shadows
made their faces blend into obscurity, but I had no doubt that
my two trackers had picked up a partner.

I sat back on the hard cushions to think. The auto was an
ancient English-made Austin that must have seen heavy taxi
duty in World War II. It certainly looked as if it had survived
the Blitz—and then had been shipped to South Africa for
retirement. The cabbie was black, looked nourished and
prosperous.

"Tell me, Johnnie," I said, glancing at the license for his
name, "how far is Cape Point?"

"Not twenty pounds distant," he said.

"Take me on a twenty-pound tour of Cape Town, then," I
told him. The smile widened. I let him wind and weave
through the quaint streets at random. I glanced out occasionally but my mind was elsewhere. The Cape Dutch houses I
saw marching by in a steady string seemed all produced by
some giant cookie cutter. Whitewashed, gabled roofs, high
front porches—*stoeps*, I corrected myself—they offered little in the way of inspiration for getting rid of my unwanted
pursuers.

The sightseeing tour palled quickly. I had the tsetse fly in
my pocket and wanted to send it to Hawk for evaluation as
quickly as possible. It appeared to be a perfect specimen,

living, breathing, flying. Yet my attacker the night before had told of carrying it in a case, turning dials and pointing sticks. None of it made any sense. I hoped that the scientists at AXE headquarters would be able to unravel the secrets and tell me what it all meant.

But to get the tsetse fly to them required a modicum of privacy. And, at the best of times, I don't like being followed. I didn't even know if my Doctor DNA was responsible or not. I wanted more information before I tackled him; slipping away from the three men following me would give me the required time.

"Let's see how good you are in traffic, Johnnie," I said, passing forward another twenty pound note.

"You in trouble? I don' run from no policeman."

"No trouble. Just in off a ship and want to see your lovely city."

"Right," he said, but his tone told me he didn't believe it for a minute. But the lure of forty British pounds was too much for him. We skidded around a corner, dust flying from the dirty street, and pounded hell bent for leather down a back alley. We emerged, turned toward Table Mountain, and broke most of the world land-speed records.

It should have been good enough. It wasn't. They followed, even more closely now so they wouldn't lose me in another bout of fast turns and breakaway bursts of speed.

"They followin' you?" Johnnie asked. "I don' want no trouble. You get out if they be trouble."

"No trouble. In fact, let them drive up alongside." I rolled the window down. Johnnie obviously thought I was going to call out to them. He slowed and the other car, a battered Citröen of indeterminate years, pulled up beside.

My Luger came up and out in one smooth motion. I saw the men inside the Citröen scrambling for cover. A single squeeze on the trigger sent a 9mm bullet into their right front tire. The car screeched into a turn and lost control.

"Take me to a nice hotel, Johnnie," I said, putting Wilhelmina back.

"Yes, sir," he said, his foot a bit heavier on the gas than before. In less than five minutes he pulled up outside a hotel. "This be one of the best. The Springbok Hotel."

"Thanks." I gave him another ten for his trouble and watched him roar off. I went into the hotel, glanced around and saw that he had picked a nice hotel—or perhaps chance dictated that a good hotel was also the nearest—and then walked briskly through the lobby and out the back. I took my time walking around the block so that I had a good view of the front door to the Springbok. Less than a minute elapsed before the Citröen, its front tire changed, clanked into view. The two men who had started this escapade dashed into the hotel, then came out again, shaking their heads. One pointed down the street toward me. I didn't move from my position in a recessed shop doorway. Then his partner pointed in the opposite direction. They finally both piled back into the Citröen and swung around, heading down the street in the direction of the harbor.

Satisfied that they'd missed me, I went back into the Springbok and registered. This would be the last place they'd look for me now, especially after being told I'd simply walked in and went through the lobby and out the back way. The room clerk eyed me suspiciously, demanded payment in advance and gave me a gimlet-eyed stare all the way to the elevator. If the men came back, the clerk would be able to give them the lowdown on me.

I didn't think they would retrace their steps.

At least not until I had a chance to take a nice, hot bath and get the fish smell off my hands and out of my clothes.

The hotel room interested me from several different aspects. The view of Cape Town was superb. I saw both Table Mountain and the harbor from the seventeenth floor. The flowers blooming like madness all over the slopes added a beauty to the surroundings not noticeable from the lower elevations. But the room itself was magnificent. I'd figured the clerk would shuffle me off to a broom closet, no matter how much cash I flashed under his nose. I still dressed and smelled like a sailor. Polluting the atmosphere of his precious hotel would have been the last thing he would have wanted.

Yet the room was luxurious, the walls hung with hides of zebra and some species of antelope I didn't recognize, and over the bed hung a wildebeest head, pronged horns jutting in a most Freudian manner upward and outward. The rug was deep pile and the tackiness I'd come to expect in most American hotels was lacking. This was a hostelry in the finest European sense.

I sighed when the phone rang. The jangling of the bell matched my nerves at the moment. I had no idea who had followed me so carelessly, but I meant to find out. The phone call might mean they'd tracked me down again—but if they had, why call in this manner? Why not just kick in the door? Surely, even the thugs in South Africa weren't as genteel as this room?

The room clerk's voice sounded, aloof and cool as I answered. Another surprise. Since I'd checked in without luggage did I want the hotel clothing store to send up a selection for me. I told the man my size and hung up, whistling in appreciation.

Definitely European in tone.

By the time I'd soaked the sweat and ache and stench out of my body, the clothing had arrived. And it suited me perfectly, too. I figured someone in the shop itself had done the selection; the clerk gave no indication of being a fashion plate.

"Thanks," I told the bellhop, making sure the door was securely locked behind him. I could offer adequate explanation to all and sundry in the hotel to assuage their suspicions later. It'd take me a little while to figure out which story I wanted to give them.

Deciding it was better to check in with Hawk, I sat down in front of the television set and examined it. I sighed. It was a European model, set for the European standards of power. Two hundred twenty volts, a different frequency, different raster pattern. But it hardly mattered. I wasn't after fidelity and perfect picture quality. I wanted communication.

Unhinging my left heel produced a tiny electronic gizmo that hooked into the tuner on the set. I fiddled with it, then turned on the set, did one more adjustment, and got AXE Headquarters immediately.

I often wonder if Hawk is a permanent fixture in his office. No matter what time of day or night I call, he always seems to be plunked down firmly behind that immense desk, like a spider in the middle of his web. He had one of his long, black, smelly cigars firmly clamped in the corner of his mouth. The only thing out of place was the way he dressed.

Jogging clothes?

I had to ask.

"The President wants all of his executive force to remain fit, N3," Hawk said glumly. "I've been out jogging a couple miles when I have the time."

"It's good for you, sir," I said, amused. While Hawk is hardly out of shape—I hope I'm in as good a shape when I'm his age—I couldn't help needling him a little. He was totally devoted to his job and taking time out for eating and sleeping galled him. If the AXE scientists ever figured out a way of going without sleep, Hawk would demand to be the guinea pig testing it. Then when I called, he'd be sitting wide awake at his desk, an intravenous needle stuck in his arm for sustenance and his fingers working madly on a dozen different projects.

"What's good for me doesn't concern you, N3. Report."

I did, as succinctly as possible. I finished, saying, "I'd like to get the tsetse fly analyzed so that I have some idea what I'm up against."

"This is the break we've needed, Nick. We had suspected this Doctor DNA, as the native called him, used insects to carry his diseases but we had no proof. Doctor DNA," Hawk mused, rolling his cigar to the other side of his mouth. A tiny cascade of ash dropped onto his sweat shirt; he never noticed.

"It tells us the man's got an overweening ego," I said.

"And it also tells us how he's creating these diseases. Recombinant DNA."

"What do you know about recombinant DNA techniques, Nick?"

"Not much," I admitted. "I hung around with a lab tech at Stanford for a while."

"Hmm," he said, glancing down at the computer readout screen embedded in his desk top. "Yes, Anne King. She received her Ph.D. last May and now works for one of the genetic engineering companies in San Francisco." He glanced up. "Do you want to hear more?"

I cursed under my breath. Being a spy makes one privy to a lot of information; it also eliminates all private life. I didn't doubt for an instant that Hawk could summon up every word said between us, even the intimate ones. Perhaps especially the intimate ones. He trusted me implicitly, but that didn't keep him from keeping tabs on my behavior. I'd been on a very sensitive mission when I'd met Anne, with the slightest slip of information being very hazardous to national security.

"No, thanks, sir. I remember what happened between us. I also remember her saying that the lab equipment to perform the gene splicing in a plasmid wasn't very complicated. All the work came in finding the proper gene to transplant."

"Essentially correct, N3," he said, shifting back to my codename. "This is of top priority. We cannot have anyone able to blackmail a government—any government—in such a fashion. Whether this Doctor DNA has come across a new technique by accident or hard work is immaterial. He must be stopped."

"Genius is my guess, sir," I told Hawk. "Three different diseases says that. If it had been just one, then perhaps accidental discovery would have been a possibility."

"Quite so, quite so," he mused. But the man's mind had already come to those conclusions. He worked through avenues of attack, ways of solving this problem as expeditiously as possible. "Your cover is definitely blown. What will it take to mend it?"

I shook my head, tapped out a new cigarette banded in gold with my monogram on the filter, then lit it. By the time the soothing smoke hit my lungs, I had a new battle plan formulated.

"The hotel knows I'm no mere sailor. I can cover my tracks here by turning into Nick Carter, ace reporter for Amalgamated Press and Wire Services."

"Very well. You are covering . . . a news conference set for tomorrow on regulating international shipping."

"Done," I said.

Hawk sighed and said, "Still, that cover as seaman was useful. We need to know where the metals this Doctor DNA extorts are sent. You got no hint while working at the docks?"

"None. There are so many ships in the Cape Town harbor at any given time, it might not be possible for me to stumble on the one carrying the strategic metals. The entire coast of Africa is crawling with cargo ships hiring out to smuggle any kind of contraband you care to name. Guns are the preferred cargo since they're easy to load and unload, but if the price was right, I think you could move the Victoria Falls on one of those tramp steamers."

"Your cover as reporter will enable you to continue snooping around the dock area and asking questions. You've been sent by Amalgamated Press and Wire Services to cover South Africa's position on territorial waters. Many countries want to extend out to two hundred miles. Ask the sailors about this, ask anyone—and keep looking for the ships carrying the extortion payoff."

"I'll try to find out how the ore's being transferred to the docks. And by whom."

"Good."

"I'll put the tsetse fly in the mail right away." By "mail" I didn't mean postal service mail, but a select courier service run between embassies. The next diplomatic pouch on its way to Washington would contain my tiny bottle and the still mad and buzzing fly.

"One other thing, N3."

"Yes, sir?"

"Find out the source of the leak. Only the usual people in this office know your assignment. I find it difficult to believe anyone has broken security at this end."

"I didn't go around advertising myself, sir."

"I know that, N3. It's possible that you were identified by accident. Your face has become rather well known over the years."

There wasn't anything I could say to that. I have files an inch thick in KGB Headquarters off Dzerzhinsky Square in Moscow. My file with the GRU is even thicker, and our "allies" have as complete a dossier as the Soviets. Sometimes the best interests of the United States don't coincide with those of our friends. It helps to know who all the players are in the game. My blown cover might have been an accident, but it had to be more than that. Another agent—friendly or otherwise—had spotted me. What was his mission? Or was it a she?

I nodded to Hawk and unhooked my transmission device. The set returned to normal commercial programming and the communications satellite spinning above South Africa freed the priority channel I'd requested.

Falling back on the bed, I stared up at the ceiling past the horns sticking out and considered my next move.

I decided to get something to eat.

The Amalgamated Press and Wire Services credentials came in handy. Hawk had already done the groundwork needed to establish me as being legally in the country. For a place like the Union of South Africa, that was nothing less than respectable work. Everyone carried travel papers, work papers, paper papers. The ultimate weapon of destruction in the Union would be a ray-gun that destroyed paper.

I went to the morning news conference in the Hall of Ministers. The building, like so many in Cape Town, seemed left over from a simpler era. The Dutch farmers—the *boers*—responsible for so much of the construction in this part of the country had limited architectural taste. Still, I suspected most of the money allotted for public edifices went to Pretoria or Johannesburg. Cape Town was an important port but it was only one of the three governmental centers of the Union.

The walls were whitewashed, the corridor a beige marble and the paintings on the walls cheap imitations of Dutch masters. As I walked, looking for conference room twenty-three, I began to wonder if the marble itself might not be imitation.

I found the conference room, presented my credentials to the everpresent armed guard, and started in. A heavy hand descended on my shoulder.

"Pardon, but I do not recall having seen you here before."

The man still holding my shoulder in what could turn into a bone-crushing grip at his slightest whim was a full three inches taller than me and outweighed me by at least fifty pounds. I saw nothing to hint that any of the surplus weight was fat.

"I'm Nick Carter, Amalgamated Press and Wire Services," I said, sticking out my hand. He'd either have to release his hold on my shoulder and shake my hand or ignore my overture of courtesy. I hoped he'd shake hands. He was starting to cut off the blood flow in my arm.

"Peter van Zandt," he said, choosing to destroy me with a piledriver handshake. I'd learned the trick on avoiding this a long time ago. It's not in outmuscling the other guy. I rammed my hand forward until the web between my thumb and index finger crushed into his. In this position, with enough forward pressure supplied by my upper arm, my hand was relatively safe from being squashed. I saw this didn't please Herr van Zandt.

"You must be the press secretary," I said. The man's manner left few other positions for him to fill.

"I've not heard of Amalgamated Press and Wire Services. Tell me about it."

"Small, but worldwide. We have our headquarters on Dupont Circle in Washington, D.C."

"Been a correspondent long?"

"A few years," I answered cautiously. "How about yourself? A minister's press secretary seems a lofty position for you." He stiffened. I smiled disarmingly and added, "For one so young."

"I'm forty-six," he said, his voice lowering a half octave. I wasn't impressed.

"Perhaps you can give me the real rundown on what's been happening." .

"What are you talking about?" His face blanched under his ruddy complexion. I felt as if I was a nasty old man who'd just popped the kid's birthday balloon.

"Why the Minister of Shipping has been making noises about South Africa extending the territorial waters out to two hundred miles. A lot of countries are trying to enforce that, in spite of the United Nations mandate that twelve miles be the uniform distance."

He relaxed. I made a mental note to check up on Herr van Zandt.

"The Union does not recognize action by the United Nations. We are only trying to prevent the unpleasantness that has occurred in other nations when foreign vessels attempt to fish inside our rightful territorial waters."

"If you extend two hundred miles, that makes going around the Cape of Good Hope a bit difficult, doesn't it?"

"We will never impede international shipping, as long as it is peaceful shipping."

"Well said," I told him, making a production of taking a spiral notebook from my pocket and running a few doodles down the margin. "Does this apply to shipments of strategic metals?" Again the strong reaction. This time I couldn't tell if it came from some guilty knowledge or whether it was simply a touchy subject in general. It could easily have been the latter.

"I must announce the minister," said van Zandt. "Good

meeting you, Mr. Carter.''

"And you, Herr van Zandt." He favored me with a dark scowl, then walked to the front of the room and mounted the dais.

I debated over sitting up front where I'd have a good view of the stage or choosing a seat in the rear of the room where I could watch all the other reporters. The matter decided itself; the chairs up close were all taken. I found one on the aisle about three quarters of the way back. Settling down, I waited for the show to begin. It started a few minutes after the minister walked into the room.

Van Zandt introduced Shipping Minister, Dieter Karlik. Karlik was a small, mousy man completely dwarfed by van Zandt's bulk. From the way the two positioned themselves, it seemed that van Zandt was the one in authority. Then I reconsidered. It looked that way unless van Zandt's job was one of bodyguard rather than press secretary. He kept his vast body between the reporters and Karlik until the shorter man stepped behind the podium.

The man leaned forward, barely able to see over the top. This was apparently the way they wanted it because Karlik made no effort to make himself visible to the reporters.

The speech itself was delivered in a high-pitched, halting voice. If it hadn't been so unpleasant, I might have fallen asleep. As it was, I felt like a school kid being subjected to the teacher dragging fingernails across the blackboard as punishment.

The minister's talk centered on new South African attempts to police their territorial waters. I couldn't have cared less about this. My gaze slowly worked around the room, taking in my fellow journalists. They were as bored as I was, except for one man sitting in the far corner of the room. He had a fancy videotape camera with a slender microphone boom attached. Wires ran down into a case at his side. He was entirely engrossed in his picture-taking, or so it seemed.

I didn't hear any whir of working motors. The new videotape cameras are all electronic, but somewhere in that case had to be a motor-driven tape transport. I shifted seats, moving closer. He didn't even notice. His attention was fixed totally on Minister Karlik.

The photographer had a head of bushy soft brown hair, well groomed, with just a hint of gray at the temples. Medium height, a little paunch around the middle, nondescript clothing, he blended into any crowd perfectly. Which made him even more suspect. The other reporters were as close to being shoddily dressed as permissible. They were used to banging around in tight areas, wallowing in dirt and then having to attend press conferences such as this. Most were presentable, but little more.

Still, I'd seen photographers and reporters who wore Gucci shoes and Bill Blass blazers.

What I couldn't get out of my head, though, was the lack of noise from the videotape unit.

It was almost as if my thoughts were telepathically conveyed to the video machine. A tiny buzzing sounded, electronic and oddly familiar. I thought for a moment, then heard the other buzzing, natural and also familiar.

I'd heard them before aboard *The Easy Ride* the night the Bantu tried to kill me using the tsetse fly.

Minister Karlik continued to talk but now and then swatted at a bug dive-bombing him. I half rose to my feet to shout a warning. It wasn't needed. Van Zandt moved with a speed that told me he was, indeed, a bodyguard and not a press secretary. One meaty fist smashed hard at the offending tsetse fly as it alighted on the podium. Van Zandt missed.

Karlik stepped back, his face twisted in fear. Never have I seen a man so frightened. It wouldn't have surprised me if he'd died from a coronary then and there. But the tsetse fly got to him first.

He screamed, swatted and mashed the insect against his neck. Karlik stood for a moment, face whiter than any newly bleached sheet, then sank to his knees. Van Zandt supported him until he lay prone on the stage, then yelled for an ambulance.

From off to the right, a small, thin many carrying a medical bag rushed onto the stage. He dropped beside the stricken Karlik and began loosening collar and cuffs, doing all the usual doctor-type things. While this interested me, I was more interested in the reaction of the reporters gathered.

All were scribbling like mad and trying to force their way from the room at the same time. Getting the story onto the wire counted most for them, even though they might not be sure what the story was yet.

"Everyone stay calm. Do not leave the room," called out van Zandt. His voice boomed like thunder. The reporters froze in midstride and turned to face him. "The minister has been taken ill, nothing more. Please remain seated."

The doctor at Karlik's side worked hard, sweat pouring off his face. I heard him mutter to van Zandt, "Where's the ambulance? I can't do a thing for him here. We *must* get him to the hospital."

"What's wrong with him?" asked a reporter from the other side of the room.

"Nothing serious, I assure you," said van Zandt. "Minister Karlik has been working long hours and is exhausted."

"He's dead," said the doctor in a shocked, stricken voice. "He's dead!"

In the distance came the undulating whine of sirens. Too late for Minister of Shipping, Dieter Karlik.

"What'd he die of?" asked another reporter in a hushed tone.

"Yellow fever. I think he died of yellow fever," said the doctor. "And there was nothing I could do to stop it. It . . . it was too fast! The disease ate him alive!"

"Doctor, please, you're speculating," snapped van Zandt. "As soon as we get the minister to the hospital, we'll release a news bulletin."

"Bloody good that'll do the bloke," came a heavily accented voice. "He's snuffed it. Some exhaustion, eh wot?"

I pressed against the back wall, studying the audience. The minister had obviously died of some disease—might as well call it yellow fever—in a very few minutes. The tension prior to the conference had been like a living being, writhing and jerking. The minister had known something was going to happen, or at least something had been threatened. The presence of a bodyguard and doctor told that.

Doctor DNA had struck again.

I wanted to talk with van Zandt and find what particular bit of extortion had been asked of Dieter Karlik, but that could wait. Someone in the room had released the tsetse fly.

And I knew who it was.

Remembering what the Bantu had said—he'd been trained to turn the dials and point the stick—I searched for the photographer with the videotape unit. It didn't surprise me to find he had vanished.

I cast one last look at the dais. Van Zandt stood as if he'd been hit with a ton of bricks.

CHAPTER THREE

The guards started to seal the room. I decided this was the perfect time to get out. Slipping between two of them in the confusion wasn't as difficult as it might have been had the men been thinking straight. The sight of the minister killed in front of them in such a grisly way had short-circuited their usual well-disciplined behavior.

In the hallway I walked with short, quick steps until I got to the front portico. Minutes, perhaps seconds, remained until the police had the entire building cordoned off, sealed up tight. I scanned the street for a sign of the photographer and his videotape case.

Nothing.

Cursing under my breath, I walked down the steps trying not to run. In a country where police expected and reacted automatically to a running man, I'd find myself in the slammer faster than light if I gave in to my natural instincts. I made it out to the street and again looked in all directions.

Behind, at the head of the steps leading to the Ministry, police swarmed like ants from a hill. I had to get out of there or be swept up.

I chose to walk south down the street and toward the harbor. No reason, just a snap decision. And it paid off. Seldom in the spy business will random guessing work. I don't believe in coincidence, but the bit of luck that revealed the brown-haired man with the videotape unit was definitely Fairy Godmother Department work.

The bustle of the morning crowds in Cape Town worked for and against me. The man stayed on foot, which was good. The press of the crowd hid me from him. No matter how often he'd glance back, I would be just another face in a huge crowd. On the other hand, if he got too far ahead of me in this crush, he'd be gone. I could never make my way forward fast enough to pick up on him if he decided to make a run for it.

He didn't appear to be in any hurry. While he didn't dawdle and gaze into the shop windows, he didn't run, either. I moved closer, trying to get some idea of where he was headed.

The layout of Cape Town is well planned. The streets are straight and run in a grid pattern around the government buildings and dock area. Out toward Table Mountain the streets turn into paths and begin to meander. My quarry changed directions and headed toward the hills. By the time he got into a taxi, I was ready for him. I'd spotted a cab of my own, and we took off in merry pursuit.

"Hey, man, this be police business, yeah?" asked the cabbie. He obviously didn't like the prospect of being caught in the cross fire if things got bad.

"No, it's a joke. A bet, really," I said, improvising. "My friend and I watch a lot of movies. He bet me I couldn't find a cab driver good enough to trail him through Cape Town."

My driver chuckled at that. "I'm the best they is. Lemme show you how good." The cab speeded up and I settled back in the cushions, my eyes intent on the cab ahead of us. I tried to figure out where we were headed. Somewhere up the coast.

The entire band between ocean and mountain is fertile farmland and heavily populated. Like the east coast of the U.S., there's not much indication when you leave one city and enter the next. The houses flowed together in a smooth band and only occasional signs indicated that we'd left one township and entered another.

"You American?" asked the driver. I had to admit I was. It was part of my cover being a reporter. "Well, man," he told me, "you in for a pleasant surprise."

"I don't like surprises," I said, my hand resting lightly on Wilhelmina's checkered grips.

"This good one. See those? The flowers? Those are the proteas. Just about the prettiest thing around the whole damn place."

The flowers he pointed out were the size of grapefruits and had a pincushion center with petals surrounding it.

"Nice," I said. I wished I'd gotten a cabbie less inclined to give me the tour and more interested in driving. I leaned forward and placed a hand on his shoulder. "On the road ahead. What's that?"

"A roadblock. Police checking papers. We near a location."

My quarry had stopped and gotten out at a small pub this side of the road block. I ordered the driver to stop and let me out.

"You don't like the police?" he asked. His smile broadened. "Neither do I. Five pounds, three," he finished. He nodded and left happy when I gave him a ten in way of thanks and told him I'd won my bet. I doubted he would report having trailed another cab, at least not until it no longer mattered.

I entered the pub and stopped to allow my eyes to adjust to the dimness. When I finally saw clearly again, I walked to a corner booth. My quarry sat with his back to the door and hadn't noticed me enter. I ordered a lager and sipped it slowly. Then came the hardest part of my job—the waiting. Trailing him to this spot had been an adrenaline rush for me. I felt that all the answers were at hand. But now I had to let

things take their own course, sit, wait, and wonder if I'd
made any bad errors along the way.

This had been too easy. I ran over the events in my head,
then decided it hadn't been that easy. I had been ahead of van
Zandt and the other guards at the Ministry in knowing the
general mechanism for releasing the tsetse fly. Karlik had
been killed in a way they'd feared, but the government still
had no inkling how Doctor DNA delivered his bugs. Something about the camera case directed the insect to its target.
Knowing this vague detail had enabled me to spot the videotape photographer and track him to this pub. It had been
easy only because I had knowledge not shared by van Zandt.

I shifted in my seat to get a better view of the camera case.
It looked quite ordinary. The man carrying it blended in well
with his surroundings. Which made him a perfect assassin.
The Bantu aboard *The Easy Ride* hadn't been a good choice.
It appeared that Doctor DNA had arranged for the first man
capable of picking up the equipment to try for me on the ship.

I grew increasingly uneasy waiting. I had no idea what the
man wanted in this pub. He sat, he drank, he didn't look
around, he didn't budge even to go to the john. The bartender
came and asked me if I wanted another beer.

"One more," I said, then stopped. Entering the pub were
eight uniformed police. "What do they want?" I asked in a
low voice.

The bartender glanced over his shoulder. "Routine crime
swoop. Looking for natives without papers, mostly. Another
lager coming up."

To him the presence of the police meant nothing. To me it
might prove my undoing. I slipped Wilhelmina and her
holster from under my arm and stuffed them down between
the stiff upright back of the booth and the seat cushion. Hugo
and his sheath followed. There wasn't much I could do about
Pierre, but it'd take a very thorough search to find him in his
tiny pouch on my inner thigh. I had barely hidden my
weapons when the burliest of the cops came over.

"Papers," he demanded.

"Good day," I said brightly, pulling out a thick sheaf of documents. "What's the problem?"

"No problem. Crime swoop."

He pawed through my documents and began to scowl. I started to get out of the booth, but a hamhock of a hand pushed me back.

"Now look here," I protested. I realized I should have kept my mouth shut. He hit me square on the chin. My legs banged against the underside of the table before I crashed down onto the tabletop.

"Anything wrong, Sarge?" asked one of the younger police.

"Papers aren't in order. Missing travel visa to get this far out of Cape Town and so near a location."

"I can explain that," I started. He hit me again. I made a bad mistake then. I lost my temper. No fat-assed South African cop is going to repeatedly hit me and get away with it.

My fist traveled less than six inches. I buried it up to my wrist in a bulging belly. The police sergeant made a whooshing sound as the air rushed out of his lungs. He hadn't even collapsed to the floor when I found myself deluged by seven others, all intent on breaking my head.

They used rubber hoses loaded with shot. Every time one of those tubes landed on an upraised arm, pain rocketed into me. I kicked myself free of the booth to stand, but by this time both of my arms were limp and lifeless at my sides from the beating. One cop swung a vicious sidearm blow for my head. I ducked enough to rob it of its full power but enough remained that it sent me reeling.

I reached out to grab myself. My arms might as well have been hamburger. Falling heavily, rolling under a table, and then reappraising my situation helped. The table kept them from hitting me long enough to regain my senses.

"Wait a minute," I called out. "Let me explain this."

"He hit Sergeant Maritz. Kill the bastard!"

Reasoning with them hardly seemed the solution right

now. They were used to dealing with recalcitrants—and with seven against one, the odds were all in their favor.

I had a chance to glance around the pub before scuttling from under the table. The bartender watched impassively, neither moving to help nor hinder. My quarry had vanished. In the back of my head ran the disturbing thought that he'd been waiting for the crime swoop before moving on. The cops would take out anyone following him and he'd have to do nothing more to cover his tracks.

If that had been his plan, it had worked to perfection.

Another hose landed on my shoulder. Pain lanced into my body until I thought I'd pass out. A foot kicked and tangled my legs. I went down again. Even though they might beat me to death on the spot, I decided I had to take that chance. There was no escaping them by fighting, of that I was positive.

"I give up!" I cried.

It was the last thing I remember saying before peering up through pain-dazed eyes to see Sergeant Maritz ponderously striding toward me. He raised a nightstick and swung it. I heard the sound as it cut through the air; I never felt it smash into the side of my head.

The world went away in a flash of red followed by blackness.

Bees had invaded my skull. Loud buzzing filled my ears and pulsating pain threatened to black me out again. I struggled to roll over and found myself up against a cold, hard, all-brick wall. My eyes eventually focused on the brick. That act performed, I rolled in the other direction and stared out into a furnitureless cell. Three others crowded into the small space with me, all of them blacks.

"They worked you over good," said the man nearest me. "You must have done something to really piss them off."

"I guess I did." I worked my back up the wall. Without its cold support I'd've fallen onto my face. I carefully examined myself and decided the injuries weren't too extensive. Puffy flesh greeted fingertips as I checked along my arms and ribs.

The rubber hoses left nasty weals but hadn't broken any bones. My face remained remarkably free of welts although a huge knot had grown on the side of my head just about the right size to be caused by Sergeant Maritz's nightstick.

"Must be plenty you done to be put in here with . . . natives."

For a moment I didn't know what he meant. Then it all came rushing back to me. This was South Africa. In the Union the worst insult imaginable was for a white to share a black's fate. Apartheid carried over into all things, including jail cells. By being put in with "natives" the police showed their scorn for me and what I'd done.

All things considered, I'd rather have been here than with "my own kind." It hadn't been a black who'd beaten me up, after all.

"How long have I been unconscious?"

"About an hour. You caught in one of the crime swoops?"

"Yeah," I said, my tongue feeling like a catcher's mitt. "What are these crime swoops, anyway? Somebody told me they were intended to catch people without papers. I had papers—or thought I did."

"They're for whatever the police want to use them for," said another of my cellmates. "Mostly they use them against us natives, to keep us in our place. But there are so many laws in this country, everyone violates at least one without even knowing it."

"I must have violated a dandy."

"You're an American." It came as a statement, not a question. I nodded and immediately hated myself for it. My head felt as if it would split open at the seams. "They don't usually give foreigners this treatment."

"These aren't usual times," I said.

"How is that? They seem quite ordinary to me. I leave the location, go to work in Cape Town, return at night, get paid starvation wages while my employers get rich. All quite normal." The bitterness in his voice told me why he was in here.

"You beat up your boss, right?" I asked.

"He hit me. I hit him. There is no such claim as self-defense if you're a native. I am guilty and awaiting trial."

"There's no fair trial here, then, either?"

"Not as in your country. I have studied it and frankly do not understand how your system works, but the words are idealistic enough. 'Trial by jury of peers.' Sentencing in this country is often by judge alone. It is too tedious to seat a jury, much less one of natives."

"I'm a reporter for Amalgamated Press and Wire Services," I said. "I'd like to discuss this more. I'm doing a series of feature articles on conditions in South Africa. Can we discuss this when you get out?"

He laughed. "I will not get out. My boss was very important, very rich, very influential. I will probably die on my way to prison."

I frowned. Was this to be my fate, too? My eyes darted around the small cell. A dozen escape plans formed in my head. I didn't dare fall into the easy, mindless, automatic behavior of a prisoner. Aggressive action might spell the difference between life and death now. I couldn't wait; I had to make things happen.

"Don't worry, my friend," he said. "You will walk away free. They have humiliated you enough. They dare not kill an American reporter. They are very conscious of their world image. Your death would bring thousands of your kind flocking to the Union to report on conditions here. That will never happen."

"I wish I was as confident as you are."

In a lower voice he said, "Do you truly wish to find out about conditions in the locations?"

I had no real idea what he meant by "locations" but I quickly said yes. Any information was better than none.

"On the outside meet with Sam Uwanabe."

"Who's he?"

"A leader. That is all I will say." Another of the men in the cell nudged him in the ribs. He turned and said, just loud enough for me to overhear, "So what if he is a police spy? We are all dead, anyway."

As he turned back, I said, "I'm not a police spy. But if I was and found Uwanabe, I'd be a dead police spy, right?"

His grin was all the answer I needed. Before I could say any more, I heard the heavy tramping of booted feet in the hall outside the cell. Three armed guards stopped outside, one of them carrying a ring of keys. The door opened. I sat and watched until the guard with the keys pointed directly at me and snapped, "You. Out."

"Me?" I said with mock delight. "I'm touched that you remembered me. And it's not even my birthday."

I fought to rise. My legs had turned to dough from the rubber hose beatings. But I refused to let them help me. Stumbling, I left the cell. As the door shut, I turned and waved to the three blacks still inside.

"Friends," I said in an aside to one of the guards. He gritted his teeth and shoved me along the immaculate passageway. Cells lined the corridor. I had only the briefest of glimpses into them as I staggered along. By the time we left the cell block my legs functioned almost normally. I didn't want to try running the Boston Marathon for another couple minutes, though.

"In here," said the taciturn head guard. He shoved, I stumbled.

Looking around the room didn't cheer me up. The walls were whitewashed and the single bare bulb hanging down from a cord cast a glaring light that made me squint. I sat in the single chair directly under the bulb. I didn't have to be told that this was the seat of honor reserved strictly for me.

I waited only a few minutes before three men entered. Two were in uniform, one in civilian clothes. Picking the man in charge was child's play.

"Nick Carter?" the man in mufti asked.

"Guilty as charged," I said, "of being Nick Carter. Guilty of nothing else."

"That's not what Sergeant Maritz's report said," he went

on without preamble. "You were a very naughty boy. Assaulting a police official during a routine search, failing to produce valid travel visas, those are only the first two. There's another complete typewritten page of charges. Any of them can get you a year in prison. Together, you'll spend the rest of your natural life on the work gangs."

"Am I allowed to send letters from the prison?" My question obviously startled the man.

"Why, yes, of course. Why do you ask?"

"I'm a reporter for Amalgamated Press and Wire Services. This can be one hell of a feature. Pulitzer Prize winning stuff. And Solzhenitzyn won a Nobel Prize for his work concerning the Russian gulags."

The man stiffened visibly. "Our prisons are not those of the Soviets." His distaste for the Russians matched mine, but I wasn't above using them as an example for my own ends.

"You know my name but I don't know yours. A good reporter always checks his primary sources." He stepped back so that he remained in shadow while the bright light glared into my eyes—good interrogation technique but poor public relations.

"I am Police Commissioner Stanhope."

"Well, Commissioner Stanhope, it seems that my wire service will have a great story, no matter what happens to me."

"What are you saying?"

"Kill me and that gets reported. And a dozen others will follow up on the story. If you send me off to jail on those trumped-up charges, I'll have a series that'll knock your socks off. Either way, great stuff."

"Who said anything about your dying? Or being sent to prison? This is a routine questioning. In the Union we must keep a strong vigilance to cut down on terrorist activities. Travel papers must match official records. Yours do not."

"My bureau chief arranged all that. He told me everything was in order." I didn't doubt for an instant that Hawk had played every conceivable bureaucratic game to insure my papers' validity. If they were counterfeit, they were better than the real thing. But South African laws being what they are, I was sure it was impossible to ever have one hundred percent up to the moment documents.

"Your bureau chief made an error. You failed to get a visa when you left Cape Town for Paarl."

"This country has the screwiest travel regulations of any place I've ever been," I declared forcefully. "Seems a white man gets treated the same as a native around here." I heard the intake of breath from everyone in the room. "I even got put in the same cell with three natives. Not even Coloreds but natives."

"An error has been made in this respect, Mr. Carter," said the commissioner. "We do not mistreat foreigners visiting our country, nor do we humiliate them."

"Maybe it was an oversight," I said slowly. Never trap a rat in the corner. He'll fight to the death every time. I had to lighten up enough so that the commissioner would let me go. The threat of world news stories concerning South African policies toward their blacks had worked miracles. Further hinting that I'd been insulted by being caged with three blacks had shown him I possessed the right type of political bent that, if he released me, no adverse stories would be written.

"What's that, Corporal?" the commissioner said. The corporal hadn't said a word. "You found the proper travel visa stuck to the back of Mr. Carter's Cape Town visa. Excellent." The man turned to me and took a step forward so that his face hovered at the edge of illumination from the bare bulb. "It has all been a terrible error, Mr. Carter. You had the proper travel permit all the time. It had gotten stuck from humidity to your other papers."

"That's a relief," I said. "Now I won't have to yell at my boss for making a mistake."

"No, Mr. Carter, you won't." The commissioner patted

me on the back like I was a longtime friend. "Did you know that the word 'boss' originated in South Africa? It's a *boer* word."

"How fascinating. An article on the contributions of South Africa to the English language might be interesting."

"I'm sure it would. Corporal," the commissioner said, turning from me, "see that Mr. Carter is on his way without any further delay."

"Thanks, Commissioner," I called, as he left the room. I couldn't see his expression. The bright light was still in my eyes.

The bartender's expression bordered on total disbelief as I walked back into the pub.

"Another lager," I ordered, sitting in the same booth I'd vacated three hours earlier.

"Didn't expect to see you again," he said, bringing me the beer. "Usually, the folks nabbed in a crime swoop are never seen again."

"I was innocent," I said.

"But you hit the police sergeant! They'd likely take you out back and shoot you for something like that. I've seen it done before."

"I'm not a native." The man's eyes widened a little as he set down the beer. Before he left I asked, "I would like to meet one, however."

"One what?"

"A native. I'm a reporter for Amalgamated Press and Wire Services." That simple statement opened up the floodgates. He understood everything with perfect clarity now. I was white; I was American; I was a reporter. No wonder I got away with defending myself from a police sergeant.

"Lots of the beggars around," he replied. "Got a location not far from here."

"What's that? A 'location?' I heard it mentioned but I don't understand the term."

"A location's where the natives live. Their homeland. The government's given them property to live on and rule for themselves. That's created quite a bit of trouble, near the borders, of course."

"Of course," I agreed. "That's why they have the crime swoops? To catch illegals sneaking across from South Africa to the locations?"

"The black beggars come out and steal and murder, then sneak back, thinking they're immune. They're not. The police are empowered to go in after them. The swoop is the best way of catching them. Sometimes they have to search entire villages inside the homeland."

"Some homeland," I said dryly. He missed the irony. "Tell me how I might get out to one of these locations."

"Most of the natives are more'n willing to show you around, if you have the travel papers to get in and out. I heard that Chief Mangope up north in Bophutatswana goes out of his way to entice tourists. He's even got himself a wave making machine."

"Wave making machine?"

"For making waves." Seeing I still didn't understand, he added, "To surf. His location is inland, not far from Pretoria, so waves are a real attraction."

"Certainly a growth industry," I said, astounded. "But I don't want to go all the way north. Anything around here?"

"You might ask down the road a way. Other than that, I can't tell you too much. No need to go into the homelands, myself."

"Thanks," I said, sipping at my beer. "By the way, what happened to the other fellow who was in here when the police came in?"

"The guy at that table?" he asked, pointing. "Don't really know. Never saw him before. Don't think he was from around here. Imagine, two foreigners in my pub in one day."

When the bartender left, I ran my hand under the seat cushions. To my relief both Wilhelmina and Hugo were there. With police searches at virtually every crossroads, carrying weapons worked against me. Still, I felt better with them on me.

I kept them under my coat until I got outside, then put them on. Crime swoops or no, I went armed.

"What's the name of the fellow you want?" the black asked, lounging back and picking his broken, yellowed teeth with a long, narrow, and very sharp knife.

"Sam Uwanabe," I repeated. "We have a mutual friend."

"Who?"

"What's in a name?" I asked.

For a long minute, the man eyed me, trying to decide. When his expression hardened slightly I knew he'd decided against the introduction. My foot looped out, caught him behind the ankle, pulled. He went sprawling, his knife clattering to the ground. I stepped on his wrist as he reached for it.

"You're not being polite. I asked for Uwanabe."

"Don't know anybody named that."

"But you were pointed out to me as a man who knew everything—for a price."

"Can't tell you what I don't know."

"And you won't be telling anyone anything if I cut your tongue out and stuffed it up your nose. I'd even use your own knife." Keeping my foot on his wrist, I bent down and picked up the knife, testing it for balance. It looked flashy but wasn't worth too much in a fight. The thin blade caused the balance to fall way back, halfway down the handle. Throwing it away would be the best way of throwing it.

"You're not police."

"I've spent the morning with the police. In a jail cell. With three blacks." My use of the word "blacks" instead of "natives" seemed to change things between us.

"You with three of us?"

"The police got confused, maybe."

"But they let you go."

"I said they were confused. I'm not. I want to talk with Sam Uwanabe. He can set the conditions. All I want is to talk."

"Sam might want to see you," came a voice from behind, "if you let that one go."

"He's too small a fish for me, anyway," I said. I dropped the knife and took my foot off the trapped wrist. Turning to face the other man, I sent my heel rocketing backward to catch the arm trying to drive the knife up and into my back. I didn't bother even looking at him. "You're Sam Uwanabe, aren't you?" I asked the newcomer.

"I've been called worse."

"Tell your friend to get lost," I said, indicating the man on the ground. "And tell him to be more careful with his knife."

"No need for me to tell him. You've done it quite admirably." The accent was unmistakably British.

"Oxford?" I asked.

"Cambridge, really, but they are ever so close except when it comes to rowing."

"You were on a crew?" If he had been he'd lost a lot of weight since those days on the Thames. Rowers need firm muscles. Sam Uwanabe was stringy to the point of emaciation. What muscle he had was piano wire, not bulk.

"Hardly. But surely you didn't risk life and limb to inquire about my sports activities? Just getting into a *bantustan* requires a certain amount of perseverance."

I had sneaked in over the border, avoiding the police patrols. The locations or homelands or *bantustans*, depending on whom you talked to, were closer to prisons than homes. I'd had an image of an Indian reservation in mind; reservations in the U.S. don't have wire fences and patrols around them.

"I need information."

"Knowledge is power," he said quietly. His dark eyes fixed on me until I felt like a bug under a microscope.

"Tell me about your group."

"Group? Do I belong to a group, as you so quaintly term it? I am a peace-loving native, nothing more."

"And as a peace-loving native, you've accumulated more scars and bullet wounds than half the allied armies in World War II." I returned his gaze, bold and almost defiant. He seemed to come to the conclusion that playing word games wasn't getting either of us anywhere.

"Why should I aid you? I doubt our goals coincide at any point. You are an American with, presumably, American ideas. Your government tacitly supports the Nationalist Party in the Union. They are our oppressors. SWAPO fights against them here in South Africa and against their puppets, the DTA, in Namibia."

I'd already run across mention of the DTA. And the Nationalist Party controlling most of South Africa wasn't far separated from the Nazis. One of South Africa's claims when appealing to the U.S. for aid was General Jan Christian Smuts' opposition to the Nazis in World War II. That was true; Smuts was an able general, but he spent as much time with political infighting in South Africa as he did fighting the Axis. Such a splitting of attention caused an otherwise effective general to be less than efficient.

"SWAPO?" I asked.

"Southwest African Peoples' Organization."

I'd heard it all before. Usually, any organization with "people" tossed into its name meant communist. But the political conditions in South Africa were such that only coalitions existed. No "pure play" politically existed. SWAPO survived through popular support, but from a portion amounting to less than half the people.

"I don't care about politics. Not in this one. I'm after information."

"As I said, knowledge is power. We wouldn't want that power to be used against us."

"I think what I want is separate. Your survival isn't threatened by my knowing about your group. Tell me. I'll report it. That's my business."

"I wonder if it is," mused Uwanabe aloud. Then he smiled and said, "I will take the chance. We need favorable world press. You will not hear anything from me that can be used against us."

"That's the only way I want it," I said earnestly. Sam Uwanabe might be a communist pawn in a game encompassing all of Africa, or he might be a self-seeking power-grabber all on his own, but I'd begun to like the man. He was the sort of leader the region needed to pull away from the fragmentation of power so prevalent. And SWAPO did fight against the Angolans and their Cuban-trained troops. They no more wanted Angolan masters than they did South African.

He began a rambling, pointless history of the SWAPO. I listened, mechanically taking notes as I considered how best to insinuate the questions I wanted answered. There wasn't any need for me to be subtle. Uwanabe gave me the information I wanted, and without appearing to know it.

"We are supplied by shipments from Cape Town into Namibia. The ships unload at points outside of Walvis Bay."

"Shipments of arms, food, supplies?" I asked.

"Those. We also smuggle contraband, reload it on ships of other nations, and obtain money to carry on."

If Doctor DNA had SWAPO aid, this explained how the strategic metals were handled. Loaded in Cape Town, shipped to some small port in Namibia, transferred to European ships, then the payoff split. The money was instantly laundered and ready for use in other ventures. No trace of the metals remained; it all went through legitimate mills in Europe.

"I've heard that your casualty rate is very high due to untrained troops. What is your survival rate after injury?"

"Higher than you might think. We have many sympathizers in the medical profession out in the veldt and rain forests."

"The old missionary?" I said jokingly.

"They haven't all been eaten by cannibals," Uwanabe

replied dryly. "While they might not support us one hundred percent, they give aid in many ways."

"Anyone in particular?"

"They do not wish their names bandied about. It is dangerous for them."

"Is there anyone who is already connected with SWAPO? I'd like to get an interview—human-interest stuff. My readers are about to the saturation point with the bullets-and-blood part of war."

"After your Vietnam, I understand," said Uwanabe. "Doctor Bron Faber is a researcher working at the Kruger Game Preserve. He has been instrumental in . . . many things. The Union government knows of his involvement but his value to them exceeds his misconduct in offering succor to SWAPO injured."

"What does he do?" I didn't know if this led anywhere interesting or not.

Then things changed.

"He is a researcher in the recombinant DNA field. I do not know precisely his interests. He has done some work with protecting endangered species on the preserve from disease. I have heard he works with insects carrying the disease. Some of the Bantus in the area even claim he supplies them with aphrodisiacs." The man laughed harshly. "They still believe ground rhinocerous horn acts in such a fashion. Do not judge all of us by a few who are still ignorant and oppressed."

"Any idea how I can find Faber?"

"He is well known on the Kruger Game Preserve." I noted that Uwanabe said Kruger as if it were "Kroo-yer." The man glanced about as if expecting someone. His entire body tensed visibly.

"What's wrong?" I didn't want him turning on me now.

"A crime swoop is in progress. You had best leave the *bantustan* before they spot you. Weapons are not permitted inside a location."

"Weapons?"

"Your pistol and your knife. For a reporter, you go well armed."

I appreciated the way Sam Uwanabe evaporated from sight. The man was in his element in the location. Like a dark mist exposed to sunlight, he simply disappeared. A haunting "I wish you luck, American agent," came down from the roof of the building behind me. I turned but was too late to catch sight of him.

I heard the police whistles, loud shouts, profanity, the sound of rubber hoses finding yielding flesh, and decided to take Uwanabe's advice. It was time for me to go.

Doctor Bron Faber was next on my list to visit. I thought I had a handle on how the strategic metals were "fenced" after leaving Cape Town. Now all that remained was identifying Doctor DNA. From what I'd heard about Faber, the two could be one and the same.

It took only seconds for me to duck down an alley and emerge in the next street ahead of the crime swoop. In less than an hour I'd crossed back into South Africa from the *bantustan*.

Somehow, the air didn't breathe any differently.

CHAPTER FOUR

After being penned up in a jail cell, crawling under barbed wire fences getting in and out of the location, and being harassed continually by police, it felt great taking a shower in the opulence of the Springbok Hotel. I ate a good meal and grabbed a short nap before reporting in to Hawk.

I fixed the gizmo on the television set and found the rapidly moving AXE communications satellite high above in its polar orbit. In seconds, the link formed between Hawk and me. This time he didn't sit behind his wide desk. I didn't recognize the location at all—the signal is patched through to Hawk, no matter where he is.

"Well, N3, what has been accomplished since we last talked?" He shifted his head slightly, and I saw a narrow hallway behind. I recognized his surroundings then. This was the hallway leading down to the Oval Office. I'd reached Hawk at the White House.

I reported quickly. Hawk nodded, made a few notes in a

spiral notebook with a black cover—I saw the red and white stripes running around the edges indicating this was a classified document—and then turned his full attention to me.

"In a few minutes, there will be a meeting of the top security advisors."

"Yes, sir, I see where you are."

"I need something definite to pass along. This matter has upset several in the government who don't like being upset." I didn't have to be told who these people were. The President headed the list, with the National Security Advisor right behind him. Perhaps even heads of other intelligence organizations agitated in the matter. While AXE and the CIA are on the same side, it often appears that we work at cross purposes. AXE takes on jobs too dangerous and too difficult for the CIA. We have a light touch and a reputation for getting the job done—fast.

"I've made contact with a SWAPO leader and gotten a lead from him."

"We are not on the best of terms with SWAPO," Hawk pointed out. "He might have fed you a red herring."

"Possibly, but I'm inclined to doubt that. My feeling is that SWAPO is willing to sacrifice certain members in exchange for better relations. I believe that Bron Faber is our Doctor DNA and that SWAPO will trade him for . . . who knows?"

Hawk scribbled furiously, then said, "This goes along with much of what we've gotten from other sources. The Cuban-trained Angolans pose a great threat to Namibia. SWAPO might want U.S. aid."

"Doctor DNA might pose a threat to them, also. He wields a lot of power. They might feel he's using them for his own ends. If the scenario I outlined concerning the metals transfers via Namibia and SWAPO is correct, they could want him removed to get a bigger piece of the action."

Hawk agreed. He glanced over his shoulder as someone out of my field of vision spoke. I recognized the voice. This was a full-fledged security meeting.

"I must hurry, N3. The tsetse fly you sent has been analyzed. Its genes have been tampered with, definite genetic engineering of the highest caliber. The fly's brain had a tiny piece of iron in it."

"Iron? It grew there as a result of the gene splicing? Why?"

"Our scientists say that the tsetse fly is now capable of homing like a pigeon or other migratory bird. The slight magnetic properties of the iron allow it to align in the fly's brain like a compass needle."

"Can it be directed using this piece of iron?" I asked. Things clicked in my mind. The electronic humming, the camera cases, the dials and the stick. The case carried a power pack, the stick was a device for magnetically guiding the tsetse fly to its target.

"There is no other reason to mutate a tsetse fly in this fashion. Who cares if a tsetse fly can find its way home over a thousand miles?" Hawk said acidly.

"What about any disease it carried?"

"A particularly nasty version of yellow fever. We must assume it is identical to what killed Dieter Karlik. Infection causes death in less than ten minutes. The internal hemorraghing is the real killer, since only a few minutes of elevated temperature will not kill an otherwise healthy man."

"Karlik bled to death inside?" I shivered. That was a nasty way to go.

"What interests our scientists most is how Doctor DNA— Faber?—has induced this virus in a tsetse fly. The normal carrier is the *Aedes aegytpi* mosquito."

"Can the South African ministers be vaccinated against it?"

"Against yellow fever, yes. Perhaps even against this viral strain. But to what end, N3? Remember the sleeping sickness and lhassa fever and green monkey disease? Doctor DNA has a potent arsenal of diseases at his command. It is impossible to guard against all of them."

"I'd better check out Bron Faber right away."

"Yes, N3, you'd best do that."

The picture faded to leave me staring at a field of white snow on the television screen. I turned off the set and began mentally preparing a cover story to present to Doctor Bron Faber.

Or was that Doctor DNA?

The Medical Research Center in Cape Town was housed in a whitewashed building just off Azalea Street. I circled the area twice to make sure of the routes in and out, having no idea at all what to expect. Finally satisfied that I could handle any problems, I walked to the *stoep*, climbed the steps and went inside.

The small office smelled of disinfectant. I felt like I'd walked into a hospital.

"May I help you?" the woman behind the desk asked in Afrikaans. She was in her late fifties, gray-haired and with a ramrod-straight posture. She would have been right at home on the paradegrounds reviewing the troops.

"I'm a reporter," I answered, also in Afrikaans.

"American," she said, switching to English.

"Is my accent so bad?"

"Your clothing is of the wrong cut. Nothing I can point to, but it is different."

"But I bought it here in Cape Town."

"Perhaps, then, it's the way you wear it. What can I do for you?" She had a brusque manner, a no-nonsense way of spitting out each word. Her speech came out clipped and precise, as if she were being graded on her diction.

"I'm with Amalgamated Press and Wire Services."

"Never heard of it."

"International, out of Washington, D.C.," I continued, refusing to let her slow me down. "I want to do a feature article on Doctor Faber."

"Faber?" she asked, as if the name was unknown to her.

"Bron Faber. I've heard good things about his work in disease. The reading public loves to pick up stories about new advances."

"Doctor Faber is not in Cape Town."

I waited to hear the rest. When nothing came I prompted her. "Where is he?"

If I'd started pulling her fingernails out with pliers her expression wouldn't have been much different. She wrestled with whatever orders she'd been given and finally relented.

"He is in the north."

"Since this lovely city of Cape Town is just about as far south in Africa as you can get . . ."

"Cape Agulhas is farthest south," she cut in.

". . . Doctor Faber being north doesn't tell me much," I finished. I didn't need a geography lesson.

"He is working with the animals."

"In the Kruger Game Preserve?"

"Yes."

A long silence developed. I felt as if we were two wild beasts tossed into an arena for some Roman emperor's pleasure. We circled each other verbally, testing, probing, waiting for a show of weakness. If the Medical Research Center was on the up and up, this odd behavior was inexplicable. On the other hand, if this was nothing more than a front for Faber's more dangerous clandestine operations, it gave away too much. Either way, Faber lost.

"Questions such as yours are not normally asked in the Union," she said, momentarily slipping into Afrikaans. Back in English, she added, "This is a close society. It does not pay to be too free with information."

"I'm not with the government. Here are my credentials." I flashed a packet of documents at her. All looked legitimate; all proclaimed me a member of Amalgamated Press and Wire Services. They'd passed muster by the police. Nothing this woman could turn on them would show them to be forgeries.

"Doctor Faber has been troubled by government regulations recently," she said cautiously. "His experiments with animals have saved numerous species from extinction."

"That's the kind of stuff I want for my feature."

"His methods are being hotly debated."

"What methods? I've heard he's a hotshot in the recombinant DNA field. Doctor DNA, he's called." She tensed slightly, then covered well. I wanted to sing and shout. That nickname had been applied to Bron Faber. I was nearing the end of my hunt.

"I never heard Doctor Faber called that."

"But he's saving animals with his scientific talents. That kind of press could take the heat off. Look, this is a touchy field. In the U.S. the city of Cambridge tried to stop MIT from establishing a recombinant DNA lab. As a result, they lost out to Stanford. Advances of staggering magnitudes come out of there every day, it seems. South Africa was the first with heart transplants. Maybe Faber can recapture the spotlight in medical research, take it away from Stanford. This can be a dynamite article."

"Doctor Faber does not want such an article written." Flat, cold, very Germanic in the precision of its delivery.

"A shame. Well, since I'm here, tell me about the Medical Research Center."

She smiled. Somehow, it didn't lighten the mood in the room. Her smile still registered a forty-below on any thermometer.

"The Medical Research Center is a nonprofit group dedicated to the betterment of mankind. We provide free medical assistance to anyone needing it. Our staff is the best trained in all of South Africa. We even have branches in Johannesburg and Pretoria."

"Doctor Faber is the founder?"

"Yes."

I felt as if a door had been slammed in my face. Knowing I'd gotten all the information I was likely to—and it was damned little—I left to return to the Springbok Hotel.

Bron Faber was north. Maybe on the Kruger Game Preserve. He had founded the Medical Research Center. It provided a nice cover for travel from Johannesburg to Cape Town and gave him a reason for shipping items in and out of the country marked as medical supplies. His work on the

Kruger Game Preserve allowed him some freedom of movement in a country obsessed with restricting travel.

I had a feeling about Faber. He was the one I wanted.

Between Cape Town and Johannesburg, I changed from a
correspondent for Amalgamated Press and Wire Services to a
medical technician and paramedic. The reporter cover had
run its usefulness. To get close to Faber through his Medical
Research Center required another sort of wedge. The woman
in Cape Town had been close-mouthed, and I had no reason
to believe I wouldn't run into even more tight-lipped people
in Johannesburg. The entire work force in the Medical Research Center might be instructed to clam up when recombinant DNA was mentioned.

Whether that came from the general mood of the country or
from Doctor Bron Faber's specific uses of his research remained to be seen. But I'd find out, one way or the other.

The airport was larger than I'd expected. Considering
Johannesburg is the largest city in South Africa, I had little
reason for the surprise. From the air, the city appeared
smaller due to the incredible sprawl of the "suburbs." The
gold mines of the Witwatersrand hemmed Johannesburg in
on three sides. Huge piles of white debris poured down
mountainsides until it appeared a perpetual snowstorm had
inundated the country. The sunlight glinted off the white dust
mounds and turned them into gigantic crystals. Not even the
sand dunes around Lake Michigan are as spectacular.

Landing at the airport was on the dicey side. Strong winds
buffeted the plane and, when I got off to walk to the terminal
and the inevitable bout with internal customs, the air was
filled with dust reminiscent of the American Dust Bowl.

I'd learned the ropes for getting through cutoms. Wilhelmina and Hugo were safely hidden. The customs men didn't
even bother using x-ray equipment. Their searches were
more thorough than any I'd ever seen before—but I'd come
prepared.

Outside the terminal, safe, and ready to find Faber, I stopped for a moment and stared at the skyline. It impressed me more from the ground than it had from the plane. The center of the city sported several skyscrapers of respectable proportions. Almost two million people squeezed into the area. Out of that population, someone had to be able to give me a lead on Bron Faber.

And someone would.

"Hey, mister, cab? Avoid the *tsotsis*."

"What are those?" I asked the cabbie. He smiled, two front teeth capped in gold.

"The gangs, mister, the gangs. They are everywhere. You try to walk in Johannesburg, you die. They don't call this *Duiwelstad* for nothing."

Devil City? Crime in any large metropolitan center is bad. I didn't see any reason why Johannesburg would be exempt, but to hear this man talk, a continual struggle for survival went on in those seemingly placid streets. Doubting his word, thinking he was only hustling a foreigner for an extra buck, I got into the cab.

"Take me to the Hotel Goli."

"You got the gold to stay at that place, mister? It mighty expensive."

I knew an outright appraisal of my net worth went on automatically in the man's head. The more he thought I had on me, the higher the taxi fare would be.

"Meeting someone there."

"He must be very, very rich." He slammed down the flag on the meter and roared off. The traffic on the road into the city grew heavier and heavier as we drove.

"It's a she," I lied. "And she's not too poor, if you know what I mean."

"Hey, you lucky man, mister. Lemme give you some advice. You think I'm hustlin' you over the fare; look around. Don' ever get caught out there. And lock your door."

He had turned off the main road and wound around along a

side road. I closed my eyes for a moment and mentally projected a map of Johannesburg. I knew approximately where the Hotel Goli was. This was only a slight deviation from a straight course, and one that just might be quicker. The number of cars on the other street had increased to the point where traffic jams happened every few blocks.

I glanced out after I'd assured myself I wasn't being taken for a ride—in both senses of the word. The sight sickened me. Blacks close to starving to death lined the road, hands held out for anything passed their way. Groups of youths congregated on street corners in the fashion of teen-agers everywhere. But the difference was in the way they held themselves. These weren't amateur punks; these kids had gone all the way to pro.

"This is a rich city, mister," called the driver, sweating due to all the windows being rolled up. "But two thirds are black and most all of them—us—are dirt poor."

"Aren't there any jobs? The gold mines are flourishing. Those are the richest mines in the world!"

"Hard to get jobs. Too many workers, not enough digging. Besides, many of the men don't want to leave their families."

"What's that got to do with it?"

"They work in mine, they live in compound. Like that one. Over there."

San Quentin looked more appealing. The compound had barbed wire in double banks around it, whether to keep people in or out I couldn't tell.

"Shift usually lasts three months at a mine. Then a miner gets to go home and see his family. They don't want nobody smuggling out their precious gold, no sir."

In this country, it was hard to determine who was the good guy and who was the enemy. I settled back and tried to blank out all around me. Finding Faber headed my list of priorities. In fact, it was the *only* item on my list.

Still, checking into the Hotel Goli disquieted me. This was luxury light years beyond anything I'd seen on the trip out here from the airport. I wondered if the cabbie gave all his passengers the grand tour.

The address for the Johannesburg branch of the Medical Research Center etched firmly in my mind, I set off walking in the early afternoon. I'd been penned up too long and needed the exercise. Besides that, I wanted a good, firsthand look at Johannesburg. The streets of downtown Johannesburg were filled with prosperous looking men and women, mostly white. As I walked due south, their numbers thinned and I came to more residential sections of the city. Fine brick buildings, some stone houses, all with neatly kept and manicured lawns and gardens, made me think of the ritziest suburbs in the U.S. The small parks dotting the area were miniature paradises. The flowers bloomed profusely and their odors were stronger than perfume. Johannesburg had another side to its coin that the cab driver hadn't shown me.

And Faber's Medical Research Center rested in the middle of this splendor.

Whatever else Bron Faber did, he played both ends against the middle well. Sam Uwanabe had praised him as aiding SWAPO guerrillas injured in battle. To put a clinic in this neighborhood required high fees not likely to be paid by injured Namibians.

"Well, well, well," came the clipped words of a teen-ager sitting on a low stone fence. "What have we here?"

I kept walking.

"You, I'm talking to you."

Turning to face him, I gave him a quick once over. He was sturdy, big-boned, strong. The protruding ridges over his eyes lent him a Neanderthal appearance and the stubby fingers drumming against the rock wall showed that he was keyed up. Drugs, maybe. I couldn't see if his pupils were dilated. I guessed that they were.

"So talk. I'm listening . . . if you have anything to say."

"A brave one. You talk big, bucko, for someone trespassing on Rudders' turf."

"And what's a rudder? Something to steer a boat?" I grew tired of this battle of wits. My opponent was already out of ammunition.

"Stop!" I kept walking. Only when I heard the telltale snick of an opening switchblade did I stop and face him again.

He held the blade in front of him, the butt end of the handle firmly pressed into the palm of his hand. He knew how to use the knife, even if he had picked a switchblade. Most switchblades are made of a low-quality steel and aren't much good for serious fighting. The sight and sound of the long blade flicking open at the touch of a button is supposed to scare most people into submission.

I wasn't in the least scared.

"I'm looking for the Medical Research Center," I said. For a moment, the punk's face clouded in confusion. This wasn't the way I was supposed to act. Frightened, yes. Macho, maybe. But inquisitive, never.

"I'm gonna cut you good. You're on Rudders' turf."

"You said that. What are the Rudders? Some sort of gang?"

"We're the toughest *tsotsi* around. Killed one damn big bunch of scumbags, we have."

"How nice for you. Where's the Medical Research Center? I'm a medic looking for a job."

"You can start work on yourself!"

His lunge was clumsy. The long, shiny blade passed harmlessly to my right side as I spun. With a deceptively gentle grip on his knife hand, I turned back and jerked. His feet left the ground as his arm tried to bend around on itself. I held his arm aloft as his body fell. A loud *popping* noise echoed down the silent street as his shoulder tore apart. The knife fell from lifeless fingers.

"You broke me arm, you bastard!"

"Probably only dislocated. You did say I should go out looking for patients. Want me to set it for you?"

He started bellowing at the top of his lungs. I didn't

recognize the words. A distress code summoning the other Rudders, maybe. My foot connected squarely with the point of his jaw. I broke the jawbone and shut him up. He went down in a lump.

I'd acted too late. Almost a dozen young thugs came from all over, like army ants swarming into a termite nest. I didn't see any guns. Wilhelmina stayed in her shoulder holster. I wanted to avoid a loud confrontation, if at all possible.

"Watchadotabenji?" mumbled a youth who looked like the clone of the one I'd disabled. I slowly translated to, "What did you do to Benji?"

"I'm a medic and was just passing by. I heard him call out for help. He was like that . . ."

"Lying bastard," snapped one behind me. I sidestepped as he lunged past. He tried to slash me with his knife. He was high on something, too. His coordination was off, and he missed by inches.

"Look, guys, I'm just passing through. I want the Medical Research Center headquarters. Maybe you know Doctor Faber? He runs the Center." Their reaction took me by surprise. They all backed off. They still ringed me in, but they weren't attacking. I'd take any respite while I considered the best way of getting away from the gang.

"You know Faber?" asked the one with greasy blond hair. He spoke with enough confidence for me to peg him as their leader. "You don't look like the type."

"The type?" I asked. "I'm looking for work as a medic with Doctor Faber. Do you work for him?"

"Work? He sells us *dagga*," cried the blond.

Doctor Faber's empire extended to many things. Illicit repair work on SWAPO guerrillas. Recombinant DNA research. Saving endangered species. Maybe extorting the government of South Africa out of millions worth of strategic metals using some of the deadliest diseases in the world. Now this punk said he got his marijuana from the good doctor. If nothing else, Bron Faber led a checkered and exciting life. I looked forward to meeting him.

"You boys shouldn't be out in your condition. Are all of you high?" I glanced around the circle. The ones that weren't wired out of their skulls had severe problems in other ways. All looked like killers. The vacant stare, the tensed, hyped-up movements, the sight of the knives still in their hands all led me to think getting away might prove more difficult than I'd thought.

Talk wasn't going to do it for me.

I hadn't been given the code designation of Killmaster for nothing. I move fast. Three of the punks were out on the pavement before the others knew what happened. This gave me enough time to sprint across the small park. I'd hoped the Rudders would tire fast and forget the hunt.

They didn't. They came on, whooping and screaming like savages. I remembered the black gangs I'd seen on the way into Johannesburg from the airport. The white gang intent on slicing me into bloody ribbons differed only in race.

The park was more extensive than I'd thought. Tiny streams meandered through a small stand of trees. I dived for cover there, thinking I'd double back and leave behind the six teen-agers hunting for me. They knew the terrain better than I did. One waited for me, knife held low and in front.

I didn't break stride. I feinted to the right with my body, kicked hard, and batted the knife away. A punch to the throat took my assailant out.

"There he is. He croaked Jesse! Kill the bastard. Kill him!"

I ran again, taking off at an easy lope. About the only words the Rudders knew were, "Kill the bastard!" Their education had been inadequate. Somehow, though, I knew that these kids had gone to the best of schools, had never missed a meal, and were as stinking rich as they were bored with life.

Social theory isn't my long suit. How a society generates youth gangs in the ghetto seems obvious; poverty, lack of jobs, lack of money, lead to boredom and violence. Why it works in exactly the same way at the other extreme end of the financial spectrum is beyond me. These weren't disadvantaged kids. These were upper-class youths. And all were intent on killing me because I'd walked down their precious street.

One good thing came out of my headlong flight. I sighted the Medical Research Center three or four blocks away. I considered running there and begging for asylum, then decided against it. When I presented myself, I didn't want to explain why I'd left a string of broken bodies behind me. A real medic doesn't break jaws and dislocate shoulders; he fixes them.

"Stop, you bloody bastard!" screamed the blond. He crashed into me when I did exactly as he'd commanded.

He went cartwheeling over my shoulder as I dropped into a neatly executed *seoinage*. The shoulder throw has never been a favorite of mine, but the opportunities to use it crop up all the time. Anyone with an arm flailing in the air is a perfect target. In the blond punk's case, he waved that knife wildly enough for me to slip in under it, shove my shoulder into his armpit and simply turn. The laws of physics and judo did the rest.

I turned to the blond leader of the pack, and said, "Look, idiot, I'm fed up with this. I haven't hurt any of you—not yet. But that's coming to an end fast. Either call off your dogs or I get tough."

"Get him!" screamed the blond. I broke his arm, then turned to the remaining Rudders.

They thought they had me. Even if twice their number couldn't touch me, these out-of-breath, over-eager, would-be killers thought they had a chance. Two rushed me from opposite sides. I ducked, grabbed an extended arm, and kicked backward. My heel landed in the pit of one's stomach. I twisted the arm until a howl of agony sounded sweetly in my ears. Not slowing a bit, I spun again, broke one punk's attempted stranglehold on my neck, and kneed him in the balls.

After all that, the last one still came on. I don't know

whether it was a matter of honor, stupidity, or just being stoned out of his head. It didn't matter. One on one, he didn't have a snowball's chance in hell against me. I stamped down on his foot. When he reacted, I spun, drove my elbow into his stomach, then snapped my fist back and into his face. He fell like a ton of bricks.

I glanced out over the again-peaceful park. Here and there bodies slowly writhed in pain. It hardly seemed possible a major battle had been fought and won here in the past few minutes. Both Wilhelmina and Hugo had remained silent throughout, too.

As I walked off, heading back into the center of Johannesburg, I heard police sirens. I picked up the pace but didn't run. The flaring blue lights atop the small police cars turned the darkening landscape into an eerie, alien scene. Whatever happened next, I felt safe. The police would never believe one man had done all that to a gang of toughs. They'd look for another *tsotsi*.

While the afternoon and early evening had been hectic, it had been beneficial, too. The brief workout had loosened up my muscles, I felt fit as a fiddle, I'd found the medical Research Center, and I was now ready to take on Bron Faber.

CHAPTER FIVE

Nearly getting myself sliced into prime ribs had been instructive in many ways. This city carried a strong undercurrent of violence to it that didn't surface with only a casual examination. The crime rate soared sky high and the police failed to cope with it, even with their crime swoops and their patrolling the borders of the locations.

Even the better parts of town were dangerous, as I'd found out.

It had been a smart move on my part changing my cover to medic from reporter. No one would have talked to me if I'd poked around asking a lot of reporter questions. It had been bad enough declaring myself a peaceful, noncombatant medic seeking gainful employment.

This time I took a taxi out to the Medical Research Center. As we drove past the park where I'd done battle with the gang of punks the day before, it struck me how placid it all looked.

No one would have guessed that I'd put down ten or so of a *tsotsi*.

The clinic floated along like a bubble on a peaceful pond. The tranquility it radiated came in stark contrast to the violence I knew boiled all around it. What struck me even more forcibly was the knowledge that Bron Faber supplied dope to the gangs in the neighborhood.

"Good morning," I said to the receptionist. She was everything the woman in Cape Town hadn't been. Small, petite, a green-eyed blond, she hovered on that thin edge between the stunningly beautiful and the breath-takingly gorgeous. Faber had first-class taste.

"May I help you?" Even her voice came as music to my ears. Soft, sweet, a voice that both caressed and promised. I took a deep breath and tried to settle down. This was business.

"I'm Nick Carter, a medic from England. I hoped I might find the director of the Medical Research Center in. I'm applying for a job."

She never batted an eye at my claim of being from England. I put on just enough of a British accent to make it credible.

"I'm sorry," she said, glancing up at me. "We . . . we don't need any paramedics at this time. If you'd only come last week. Doctor Faber needed an assistant for his work out on the Kruger Game Preserve."

"Doctor Faber?" I said. "Is he the head man?"

"Yes, and such a fine doctor," she said. My estimation of her dropped a little. The obvious hero worship in her voice told of a crush on the man. I didn't even know what Bron Faber looked like and already I had him marked as a deadly enemy. I'd hope this lovely blond would have seen through his façade to the darker side of his nature.

Then again, I still didn't know that Faber and Doctor DNA were one and the same. I simply assumed it.

"I've heard of his work. With endangered species. It must

be interesting working with a man who's sure to be nominated for a Nobel Prize one day.''

"You think he will? Oh, he *so* deserves it," she gushed. She leaned back in her swivel chair. The crisp starched white uniform did nothing to hide very womanly curves. The day was a bit hotter than the weather forecast had predicted, and she wore the uniform unbuttoned a very unnurselike two buttons to reveal a warm surge of breast. The woman seemed oblivious to my examination of her, so great was her enthusiasm for Dr. Faber.

"Even in England we've heard of his recombinant DNA work. With insects, wasn't it?"

"Insects and diseases of the animals in the park. He's isolated several of the most virulent strains. And . . . oh, I'm not supposed to mention his work." She actually blushed. It had been years since I'd found a woman who blushed.

"Why not?"

"He is such a modest man. He doesn't like to boast or carry on about his contributions."

"But they're such big contributions!" I protested. "The genetic engineering work has altered tsetse flies to be able to control them."

"You've heard about that? Oh, marvelous. In a paper? He's finally released that to the scientific journals?"

I nodded and went on.

"And look at these clinics. The Medical Research Center in Cape Town does wonderful charity work."

"We do here, too, though we're some distance from the nearest location," she said solemnly. She really believed everything she said. You can fool some of the people *all* of the time. "It's difficult getting into the locations outside Johannesburg. Chief Kaiser Mantanzima . . ."

"Mantanzima?"

"In the Transkei location for the Xhosa," she quickly explained. It didn't do me any good. "The Chief positively refuses to allow us in to examine his people. Disease is rife there. It's awful.''

"I know something else that's awful," I said.

"What's that?"

"We've been talking for almost five minutes and I don't know your name." Again she blushed. I thought it made her even prettier. It also made me wonder how she'd respond to an indecent proposal. I suspected she would stare in confusion and disbelief, then decide no one could be so crude as to assume that two consenting adults ever *did* that.

"I'm Erica der Klerk." She stood to shake hands. I took another deep breath and wished for a cold shower, too. Her white-stocking encased legs more than matched the perfection of the rest of her body. I found it increasingly difficult to keep my mind on Bron Faber. Maybe the man planted such a lovely blond lady out front for just that very reason.

Erica der Klerk proved an excellent diversion.

"Most pleased to meet you," I said, sincerity ringing in the words. "And I'd really be in your debt if you could tell me where I might find a job, if Doctor Faber isn't hiring right now."

"Well," she said, her gaze growing bolder as she studied me, "Doctor Faber has his assistant for the Kruger Game Preserve, but we might need some help around here. I do hate to bother him about such things. I'm supposed to be the office manager."

"You're not a nurse?"

"I am, but I hardly ever get a chance to use my skills," said Erica. "So much happens here that I seldom get to actually work with the patients."

"Paper work, you mean?"

"That is awful," she said, laying a delicate hand on my forearm. As if she realized she'd taken some liberty, she pulled away as if scalded. I hadn't minded at all. "But," she continued, "the ordering, the shipping, the day-to-day operation and coordinating patients and doctors is what takes the time.''

"Shipping?" I asked lightly.

"Nothing much," she said. I thought a tinge of blush colored her cheeks again. "Doctor Faber ships a lot of material between Centers. We're the largest here in Johannesburg, but the Cape Town facility handles overseas deliveries."

"And outgoing shipments?"

"Why, yes. Lately we've had a considerable amount of medicines going to Namibia."

There wasn't any way to disguise metal ore as medicine, unless Faber managed to get the permits and official documents, then alter them to get the strategic metals out of the country. With the hold he had on the various ministers, I doubted he needed to do too much fancy shuffling around. And then again, perhaps he didn't want the ministers he threatened to know the destination of the shipments.

"I certainly admire Doctor Faber's setup here."

"You do, eh?" came a deeply resonant voice from behind. I turned and faced a man slightly taller than me and weighing ten or fifteen pounds less. The name tag on the white lab coat read "Faber."

This was my man.

All I needed now was concrete evidence that he was Doctor DNA.

"I certainly do, Doctor Faber. And I'm not just saying that to get a job."

"Wouldn't hurt if you were." He smiled disarmingly. I thought I could like him a lot. His warmth and outgoing manner lulled any suspicion I had of him. Yet the pieces to this deadly puzzle were too sharply defined, too precise, too damning. While it was all circumstantial evidence mixed in with a lot of guesswork on my part, I'd bet my life he had killed at least four South African ministers of state and had sent the Bantu to kill me aboard *The Easy Ride*.

To kill with virulent diseases long thought under control.

I repressed a shudder at the memory of Dieter Karlik burning with fever—and bleeding to death internally from the yellow fever he'd been infected with.

"Your Ms. der Klerk has painted such a glowing picture of your work that I'd be tempted to volunteer my services."

"But?" he prompted, hazel eyes twinkling.

"But I'd starve to death. I really do need a job that pays."

"We can't offer much, but room and board can be part of the deal. Would that suit you?"

"Yes!" I didn't need to hide my enthusiasm. To be able to stay here on the premises proved an extra bonus.

"Do you have a medical degree?" he asked. "I need to know how much work I can squeeze from you."

"I had two years of medical school, but the expense drove me to find work. I couldn't earn enough to pay for tuition without working hours so long that studying became impossible."

"So you've had two years. What else?"

"I worked as a paramedic for several years in New York City."

"That explains the slight trace of American accent."

I was happy I tossed in that part about working in America. Faber was no one's fool, whether he was Doctor DNA or not. I've run across border patrol officers who can tell every place a person has lived simply by listening to a few sentences. Their skill borders on the uncanny. In a country like South Africa where so many foreigners come and go due to the extensive mining operations, the locals developed a good ear for accents, too. Faber's ear was better than most. I'm good when I put on an accent; the British pronunciations came easily to me, also. In spite of that, he'd picked out the faint remains of American English.

"Can't say I'm happy you picked up on it. My time in America was not the best of times for me."

"Oh?" he asked, arching an eyebrow. "Why not? I've found the United States a pleasant enough place the few times I've been there."

"The people," I said without hesitation. "They have such odd ideas politically."

"Well, yes, there is that," he conceded. "But top-notch medical facilities. Let's go check out a few patients and see how you do."

"Thanks, Doctor Faber."

"Don't thank me yet. I haven't hired you. But you might do nicely, if your medical skills are honed properly."

"I think he will do marvelously," piped up Erica der Klerk.

As Faber and I went into the back of the clinic, I flashed the blond my most winning smile.

"This clinic doesn't have the emergency cases the Cape Town Center does. I cater mostly to the neighborhood problems."

"Such a fine neighborhood," I said. "Looks very prosperous. Hard to believe there are problems of any sort here."

"There are," he said, a touch of grimness entering his tone. "Drug addiction is rampant. The well-to-do children are bored. They have too much time and money. Rather than channel their natural energies into constructive areas, they buy drugs and experiment with them."

"Do you handle many natives here?"

"I go out to the location once a week, when I'm in Johannesburg. Sad out there, very sad. But no, we don't see many natives."

I hoped that I wouldn't have to perform anything beyond my first-aid training skills. The examination room was compact and probably well stocked with drugs and equipment. I didn't know. AXE trains its agents to patch themselves up enough to keep going until the mission is completed, nothing more. I've closed my own wounds with staple guns and even epoxy glue. I doubted if Doctor Faber would approve of those as even rough-and-ready first-aid techniques in his sterile clinic.

"It seems, Mr. Carter, that my patient has flown the coop. The old gentleman was sitting here waiting for me when I went to speak to Miss der Klerk. We'll have to postpone your examination for, hmmm, about an hour until Mrs. Vorster comes in. I'll be around. Just acquaint yourself with the facility.'' I felt a surge of paranoia. He had used my name. We'd never been introduced. He must have been eavesdropping on the conversation I had with Erica der Klerk. Faber left me wondering if he suspected I was more than a simple paramedic. He'd given me carte blanche to snoop around. Did he intend for me to use that freedom to dig through drawers and seek out damning evidence?

Did such evidence even exist here?

I compromised by looking over the room, trying to impress details on my mind. I also made every effort to find any place that might conceal the evidence needed against the man, but didn't pry too far into them. That would come later, when I was sure I was alone.

A tiny moan rattled from the far closet. At first I thought I'd mistaken the soft breeze blowing for a human sound. When the moan came again, I knew I wasn't wrong. Opening the closet door produced an unexpected result. A man about sixty years old fell out backwards to sprawl onto the tiled floor.

His face was gray and his breathing nonexistent.

''Doctor Faber!'' I shouted, dropping beside the man on the floor. ''Doctor Faber!''

I immediately began mouth-to-mouth resuscitation. I blew in, inflated the lungs and let the chest action naturally expel the air. I did this three times, then began work on his chest. Hard pressure over the heart, release, pressure, release.

I shouted for Faber again.

Erica der Klerk came in.

''Mr. van Riebeeck!'' she cried.

''I think he's had a heart attack. Do you know what to do?''

''Where's Doctor Faber?'' she asked.

''I don't know. Left for an hour. It doesn't matter. This guy needs help—now! And we have to give it to him. Help me.''

''Keep going on the chest,'' she said. ''I'll take over the

mouth-to-mouth." The thought flashed through my mind what a lucky stiff this van Riebeeck was. Then the pun hit me. He would be a stiff if I didn't get down to serious work.

Erica and I coordinated our efforts well. I felt feeble heart action starting and the man's breathing became ragged. His body responded to our ministrations.

Erica leaned back on her heels, her skirt pulled taut around her firm thighs. She looked like a real angel, her blond hair in disarray around her face and shoulders.

"Who is this?"

"Mr. van Riebeeck was the patient scheduled for nine. I thought he'd left."

"Faber thought so, too. I found him in the closet."

"The closet?" Erica turned and looked at the door. "God, no! He must have thought it was the water closet."

"And he had a heart attack and fell in. His fumblings to get out must have closed the door behind him," I finished. "Sounds incredible."

"Mr. van Riebeeck's eyesight isn't the best, nor is he physically strong," she said.

"We don't dare leave him alone. Can you handle him while I go find Doctor Faber?" I asked the woman. She nodded. I hadn't gotten ten feet down the hall when Faber came striding up to me. I hastily explained what had happened. He shoved past me and rushed into the room.

I'll give him this. He worked quickly and efficiently. Every order he gave us was sharp, precise, and clear. He made no mistakes. Erica got him a heart needle of lydocaine while I fitted an oxygen mask over van Riebeeck's nose and mouth. In a few minutes, the old man breathed more easily and color came back into his face.

"Miss der Klerk, get an ambulance here to transfer him to Voortrekker Hospital. They have the facilities there for caring for him." The doctor stepped back and wiped a single bead of sweat from his upper lip. Throughout, he had remained cool. The perspiration was the only sign that he'd been under any strain at all. To me he said, "You saved his life, Carter. I wanted an example of your skill. I have it. You're hired.''

''Thanks.''

''Thank you. You saved a man's life.''

''That's important in the medical field,'' I said, watching Faber closely.

''As in all things, nothing is absolute. Sometimes it is necessary to sacrifice the healthy for the greater good, but in this instance, you performed admirably.''

''Will you go with him to the hospital, Doctor?'' asked Erica.

''I'd better. Mr. van Riebeeck's condition is still unstable.''

''And he's very wealthy,'' said Erica under her breath so that only I could hear.

''You two can run the Center without me. Miss der Klerk will show you the ropes, Carter. And good work, both of you.''

With that, Bron Faber and the ambulance attendants took the stricken man out and loaded him into the meat wagon. Sirens blared and the ambulance raced off for downtown Johannesburg.

''It's been an exciting day. Usually emergencies don't happen at the Center,'' said Erica, tidying up her desk. Her fingers lightly caressed the papers and almost hesitantly pushed the work into folders.

''Do you always close the Center so early?'' I asked. It was a few minutes before five o'clock.

''Our business comes during the day. Doctor Faber, when he's in Johannesburg, will return during the evenings. I've never seen how busy it is then.''

''He handles it all by himself?''

''Of course. He's very good,'' she declared positively. I saw that Erica der Klerk had a very strong case of hero worship going with Faber. With a little luck and some smarts, I'd have her telling me all I wanted to know about the man. I wondered if she realized he came back to the Center to sell marijuana to the neighborhood gangs? As far as I could tell, the Medical Research Center existed solely to bolster Faber's cash flow. He peddled dope, he duped rich patients into paying exorbitant sums for very little—and he used the Center as a cover for his shipping activities.

I still had no concrete proof he was Doctor DNA. I'd worked my way through the clinic and had turned up nothing. The man kept very strict records of all transactions—the legal ones. In the Union, the police might seize records at any time. If Faber's illicit activities extended to extortion, he'd hardly keep records of it here in Johannesburg.

My bet was that the real evidence existed out in the veldt, out at his wildlife research laboratory in the Kruger Game Preserve.

"I'm very glad I'll be working with Doctor Faber," I said. Then, softer, "And with you, Erica. You're very pretty."

Her green eyes locked with mine. This time she didn't blush, even though it was apparent our thoughts were pretty much the same. Her breath came in short, quick pants that caused her breasts to rise and fall in the most seductive manner possible. Somehow, that third button on her uniform came undone. Creamy white breast flowed up and threatened to come spilling out.

I would've caught it. My fingers ached to stroke over those smooth mounds. Maybe it was the surroundings that got to me as much as Erica's beauty. It had been a long time since I'd played doctor.

"Wh-why don't you come back to my flat? I c-can fix us supper," she said. The slight stutter betrayed her real interest.

"I'd be delighted."

We left, hips brushing. This small friction sent both our heart rates soaring. I felt it and I know Erica did. I saw a tiny vein in her swanlike throat pulse and throb. By the time we reached her apartment, about three miles away, just on the outskirts of downtown Johannesburg, we both knew that supper would be late. After we'd finished making love.

She closed the door and spun around, slipping into the circle of my arms. I'd had Erica pegged as being the shy type. There was nothing demure about the way she kissed me. She might blush but she knew what she wanted and how to go about getting it.

Her lips parted slightly allowing my tongue to surge forward. I moved over her tender lips, then snaked into her oral cavity. Our tongues met and caressed, sliding past one another. Breath coming hard, I began flicking my tongue against the tip of hers. When our tongues began playing hide and seek, dashing back and forth, my hands began to wander.

Up and down her back I felt the crisp, starched white uniform. It had to go. I worked down to her womanly hips, felt the flare of her rump, cupped the meaty slabs, and squeezed. She moved closer, her body grinding passionately into mine.

My hands worked forward, then up. Her belt came off. Then I undid the three buttons remaining fastened on the upper half of her uniform. With a sigh, she broke contact between our mouths and stepped back.

"Oh, Nick, this is going to be so good."

"I know," I said. I didn't want conversation. My eyes worked over her body as she shrugged her shoulders. Her uniform top dropped to her waist. With a sinuous wiggle that sent waves of desire pulsating through me, she got rid of her entire uniform. It lay in a pile around her slender ankles. Erica stepped forward and away, clad only in bra, panties, garter belt, and stockings. The lady sure knew how to dress underneath. It was in stark contrast to the crisp, white uniform of moments before.

"You're over-dressed," she accused. "Let me do something about that." And she did. As her nimble fingers worked over my clothes, I unhooked her bra. The woman's conical breasts spilled forth. I held one in each hand, as if judging their weight. More than ample was my instant evaluation.

The penny-colored nipples hardened from both the sudden exposure to the air and pure, simple lust.

We waltzed around, pulling and tugging at one another. I had her bra and panties off and tried to work down the garter belt and white cotton stockings. She gently removed my hand and said, "Leave them."

I did.

We flowed together like two streams running into a larger, more vital river. Our mouths worked hard and our bodies pressed close. Erica turned into a real tiger. She was totally unlike the shy, reserved, blushing woman working in the Medical Research Center.

"Now, Nick, take me now. Do it *now!*"

There wasn't any way to refuse her. We slipped downward, gravity exerting its pull on our interwined bodies. Somehow, the bed appeared under us. It wouldn't have mattered. We were both so turned on the floor would have sufficed. I felt her stocking-clad legs scissoring on either side of my body. I was glad she had insisted on leaving them on. This was sexier than I'd have imagined possible.

Those wonderous, slim legs of hers parted wantonly. Her dextrous fingers found my hardened length and tugged me toward her center. Dampness greeted me, then warm, clinging flesh. I sank full-length into her core. We both gasped at the intrusion.

For an instant I thought she was having some kind of fit. Her body went berserk under me. But it was only need, desire, stark lust. She arched her back and rotated her hips to take my hardness all the way into her depths. With this delightful urging, my own hips began to respond. Slowly at first, then with gathering momentum. I didn't seem to be able to give her enough. Erica was insatiable.

Then, like a string pulled too taut, she broke. Her sexual peaking pushed my own control to the limit. I'd thought I could rest for a moment, but Erica wouldn't have any of it. If anything, I'd only whetted her appetite. She wanted more. And she got it.

Firm, smooth, I stroked. The lovely blond moaned and gasped, her words turning incoherent. But as she approached another climax, she grated out from between clenched teeth, "Yes, Bron, oh yes, take me. I need you, Bron my love. Yessss!"

She fantasized another lover—Bron Faber.

I finished in a rush, with Erica wildly clawing and moaning all the while. We lay panting, drenched with sweat, on the bed clutching each other.

"You're quite a surprise, Erica," I told her.

"Surprise? How is that?" She snuggled closer, her hot breath gusting through the hair on my chest. Her teeth gently nipped and bit as her tongue stroked and teased.

"This you is so different from the cool, at-work you."

"It . . . it's difficult when I'm at the Center."

"With him around?" She tensed. I held her close and refused to let her flee. She soon subsided and snuggled even closer, if that was possible.

"Yes," came a tiny voice. "I know I can never have him. But I think about it a lot. I'm not good enough for him. And now he's going to marry that bitch from the Netherlands."

"Who's that?" I asked, stroking her hair gently. Her own fingers worked much lower over my body. I felt stirrings of desire for her again.

"Alleen something or other."

"Never say that you're not good enough for anybody. You're as good as Alleen," I told her. "You might make better time with Doctor Faber if you'd relax around him."

"I can't. I've tried, but I can't."

The armchair psychoanalysis that flashed through my mind told me the sad story. Erica's hero worship of Faber prevented her from getting close to him. Instead, she went to bed with any man who came along and fantasized that he was Faber. This didn't do much for my ego, but then, exciting though Erica was, I *had* brought her here for information. A spy must use all the tools of the trade—and sometimes sex is one of them.

A great deal more than personal feelings were at stake. If I failed, no government in the world would be safe from the extortion threats offered by Doctor DNA.

"Why don't you transfer up to the Kruger Game Preserve Center?" I asked. "That seems to be where he spends most of his time. Being around would show him how much you care for him."

"This doesn't bother you, my talking about Bron?"

"Not at all, Erica. In fact, I'd love to get up to the Preserve myself. Sounds like a great research opportunity. Saving endangered species, researching diseases."

Her silence told me she was thinking, as well as playing with me. I rolled onto my back to allow her to continue both undisturbed. Erica finally said, "I can get you transferred up there, if you want."

"I'd hate to leave you, but . . ." I let the sentence hang. I had to give her the chance to make all the right decisions on her own. I was positive she thought that getting rid of me by sending me out to the veldt would be worthwhile. She'd blurted out her secret love for Faber. Get rid of me, get rid of a challenge to her fantasy world.

"You're good in bed," she said after a long time. "About the best."

"It might complicate things if I stayed around. I don't want to make you choose between me and Doctor Faber." In her mind, there could be no real decision. The fantasy lover always came out on top over a real one. I sensed that it had happened in the past with Erica der Klerk and would happen again in the future.

"It's not that, Nick. You do want to work in the veldt? It's away from civilization and Doctor Faber's researches are very dangerous."

"I want to help him however I can."

Lightning didn't strike me, which was just as well. With the blond coiled around my body, it would have gotten her, too. Her eager mouth worked all over. I moaned. I hoped she decided to put through the request to ship me out to the

Kruger Game Preserve Center soon. This was both exciting and tiring dealing with her.

"I'll see to it in the morning."

It was a long, hard night. But sometimes the life of an undercover agent is actually spent undercovers. Delightfully so.

CHAPTER SIX

It might have been my death warrant Erica der Klerk signed for all the enthusiasm she showed. With a flourish, she finished the paperwork on my transfer from the Johannesburg Medical Research Center to the research station Bron Faber maintained out in the veldt.

"I'm sorry to see you go so soon, Nick," she said softly, her eyes dewy. "It's been . . . good."

"Very good, Erica," I said, meaning it. But my mind already traveled ahead to the Kruger Game Preserve and Faber's facilities there. I'd contacted Hawk and told him of my progress. He told me to move faster. Doctor DNA had made outrageous claims against the government of South Africa and had killed three more top officials to reinforce his demands. Two had gone via yellow fever and the last had been murdered with some quick-acting disease that remained as yet unidentified, even by the experts at the Center for Disease Control in Atlanta, Georgia. The man stricken with the disease had seemed to melt, his flesh turning into putty. Along with the flesh went the nervous system. He'd virtually shaken himself to death.

Stopping Doctor DNA became even more imperative.

And I'd put all my eggs in one basket. I went on instinct as much as anything else. My hunch that Bron Faber was responsible was just that, a hunch. If this lead didn't pan out, I was back to square one. And time was running out.

"I hope you don't mind me saying what I did to you," she said suddenly. I looked into her green eyes. She blushed.

"What do you mean?"

"About Doctor Faber having a new assistant. He tells me to say that to all the people coming to look for work. He really does need an assistant."

"Maybe you should clear this with him," I suggested. "Wouldn't want you getting into trouble with him."

"Oh, no, Nick, there's no problem. I already spoke with him. He was very impressed with your quick thinking. Mr. van Riebeeck is doing nicely. They expect him to be out of the intensive care unit in another few days. He's going to be just fine, thanks to you."

Erica's words bothered me. She'd already spoken to Faber, and he'd cleared my "promotion" to assistant out on the veldt. Was this just a convenient way of getting rid of me? Who's going to question a lion about dinner? Especially if you think that dinner's been a human? Still, my job required me to go into this with my eyes wide open.

"So all I have to do is catch the Center's plane?"

"Yes, Nick. It's parked at the far end of the airport." She went back to shuffling papers, then looked up, unshed tears in her eyes. "Give me a call now and then."

"I will. And I'll let you know how he's doing." This pleased her more than anything else. Fantasies are more real than reality itself to some people.

The small plane emblazoned with the Medical Research Center insignia of the entwined DNA double helix circled the

Kruger Game Preserve airfield, then spiraled down. I blinked in the bright sunlight and tried to shake the misconceptions I had about Africa. As a kid I'd loved the old Tarzan movies, especially the ones starring Buster Crabbe. Swinging through the jungles on a vine, giving out his yell, wrestling the killer male lion—all of it was bunk.

Technically, there aren't any jungles in Africa. There are only rain forests, and in this part of the continent it's mostly dry veldt, with plains stretching to the horizon. Further to the south and west is the Kalahari, one of the most arid regions on earth. Next, the famous yell was a composite; no single man ever gave it in the movies. Finally, the male lion is almost a parasite. The female lions do the killing while the male watches and then reaps the rewards.

None of the reality took away from my feelings. Africa. Birthplace of humankind. Far to the north was the Olduvai Gorge. Zebras and giraffes and leopards and gemsbok raced those plains, animals extinct in all other parts of the world and bordering on vanishing even here.

Here also was Bron Faber's research center, miles from the nearest civilized outpost. The compound had been patterned after a native *kraal*, making it more of a family unit than a city. The few buildings all fastened together with walkways or shared walls, giving the appearance of an extended family arrangement.

The plane landed, taxied and came up to the end of the runway. The taciturn pilot gestured for me to get out. I did. He spun the single-engine plane around and took off. I was left behind in a cloud of choking dust.

"Well, some reception," I said to myself. The buildings were almost a half-mile distant. I hefted my single bag and started walking. Halfway there, a snorting noise froze me in my tracks.

I'd heard similar sounds before when I'd hunted javelina in south Texas in the hills around Austin. Those boars are the most dangerous in the world. Long, sharp, dirty fangs will rip you apart if you miss on the first shot. And sometimes even a good, solid hit with a high-powered rifle won't stop those miniature tanks. They barrel on, snapping and foaming at the mouth. A dangerous pig is hard to cope with.

Ahead of me, rooting in the dirt, was the ugliest pig I'd ever seen in my life. About the size of a boxer dog, the warthog had long, curving fangs that looked all too functional for my taste. Hairless except for a mane like a lion's, it stared cross-eyed at me. I put down my bag and loosened my jacket. My Luger was free in its holster but I hesitated making the move to draw it.

A 9mm shell has enough stopping power for most applications—it's adequate for killing a man. I doubted if even a full clip of bullets could stop a charging hog this size. Those tusks gleaned yellow and filthy in the bright African daylight. Visions of them ripping me into bloody shreds sent a cold ripple up my spine.

"Hallo!" came a pleasant female voice from further down the path. "How are you?"

Eyes fixed on the warthog, I called out, "Stop! There's an animal in the pathway. Dangerous one."

"What? Oh, a warthog? Don't worry. That's only Freddie."

"Freddie?" The warthog turned, as if confused.

"Shoo, Freddie. That's a bad boy, scaring Herr Carter like that."

I'll be damned if the warthog didn't slink off to its burrow, turn around, and then back in.

"A pet of yours?" I asked. A deep breath took the edge off the adrenaline high I rode:

"Something like that," she laughed. I got my first good look at the woman. Perhaps twenty-one, raven-dark hair, ebony eyes, a pale complexion, and a figure that promised excellence in all curves. She wore a slightly baggy safari jacket, long khaki pants, and heavy boots. A faint whiff of perfume drifted to me on the warm wind: Chanel.

"You have the advantage on me, in more ways than one.

You have mystical power over the wild beasts of the veldt,'' I said, nodding toward Freddie's burrow where only an ugly snout protruded, ''and you know my name while I don't know yours.''

''Herr Carter, I am so glad to see that Freddie didn't scare you unduly. You are too gallant.'' Her words were heavily accented. Dutch. It came as no surprise when she introduced herself.

''I am Alleen Kindt.''

''Doctor Faber's fiancée. Pleased to meet you. And I'm so happy to be here to help out your future husband.'' The way her face clouded told me that things didn't run smoothly between her and Faber. This gave me a wedge to push in further. But that would have to wait until later.

''Come into the house. Bron—Doctor Faber—is out on the veldt. He . . . he is working on his latest project.''

''The insect problem? The genetic engineering on the tsetse fly?'' I probed. She winced. I'd hit another sore spot. Things went very poorly between her and Faber.

Again, she didn't answer. The dark-haired woman called out to a native to fetch my bag.

''Chinua will get you settled.'' I thanked the woman, but it was to her back. She walked off, mopping her face with a delicate lace handkerchief.

To Chinua I said, ''I must have offended her.''

''No, she is like this much lately.''

''Why?'' A shrug was the only answer I got. I studied the native, then asked, ''Isn't the name Chinua a Nigerian name?'' That stopped him dead in his tracks.

''Yes. How do you know that?''

''I've wanted to work in Africa all my life. I read a lot. Means, uh, don't tell me . . .''

''The name means Chi's own blessing.''

For the Ibo tribe of Nigeria, each had a personal angel or guardian known as Chi.

''What are you doing this far south?''

Again the shrug. He must have learned it from an Italian. It had the same eloquence that meant everything and nothing at the same time.

"Must be Doctor Faber," I gushed on. "He's a great man."

"An ambitious man. He will conquer all of . . ." Chinua stopped in mid-sentence.

"Disease?" I finished for him. That wasn't what he meant, but he still nodded. "Yeah, Faber is a great man. The work he does with mutated diseases is of untold potential value to mankind."

"They sometimes get out of hand."

"What's that?" I cried. "You mean some of the diseases escape the laboratory?"

"I know little, but many have died since I came six months ago. They die strange deaths, some with fever, others turning almost white." The irony in his voice matched the hurt. "He says they were natural deaths, deaths to be expected in the veldt."

"But you don't think so."

"This is a nice room," he said, avoiding the question. "You will like it a lot during your stay."

"I hope it's a long stay. I'm looking forward a great deal to working with Doctor Faber." I dropped onto the bed and watched Chinua, then noticed what was missing from the room. I stopped him and asked, "Where's the mosquito netting? I don't want to be eaten alive by insects."

"You will not be. Doctor Faber doesn't allow bugs inside his *kraal*." Chinua left me thinking that over. I carefully searched the small room, looking for bugs both real and electronic. I found neither. It felt as if I'd been dropped in the middle of Adventureland in Disneyland; bugs were forbidden and didn't dare show their antennae.

The prospects for recombinant DNA were stupendous, if this control of the environment had been engineered by Faber. However, that sword cut both ways. Great good might be countered by even greater evil.

I had to find out—soon.

* * *

The common room looked as if it had been decorated by a Hollywood stage manager. Zebra skin adorned the floor and a springbok head had been nailed to the wall. The wicker chairs were identical to ones I'd seen in a hundred jungle movies and were as uncomfortable as they looked. Still, simply sitting and collecting my thoughts had much to recommend itself. Chinua brought me a drink made from undefinable liquids that tasted slightly bitter but which quenched my thirst nicely.

Staring out an open window across the veldt, I saw hilly, rocky areas in the distance.

"Those are *kopjes*," came Alleen's voice. I rose to face her.

"Please, sit down, Herr Carter. We do not demand civilized courtesies out here in the wilderness."

"You don't like it out here, do you?" The answer to that question was obvious in every word she spoke, the way she frowned as she gazed over the veldt, the very carriage of her body.

"It's not that so much," she answered. "I could like it here. Never love it like Bron, but it might become home. I just miss him so."

"His trips to Johannesburg and Cape Town must be longer than I thought. The people at the Medical Research Center in Johannesburg complain he is there all too short a time."

"Erica der Klerk?" the dark-haired woman laughed. "She has such a crush on Bron. If he were there twenty-four hours a day, three hundred sixty-five days a year, Erica would complain about missing a day every leap year."

"You two have met."

"She doesn't like me, not one bit."

"Because you took Bron away from her." The color that rose to the woman's pale cheeks reminded me a great deal of the way Erica blushed at every little remark.

"I hardly took him away from her. Bron and I met in Amsterdam six months ago. He attended an international conference on applications of genetic engineering. My father also attended."

"And you went along for the ride."

"Hardly," she said, a wistful sound in her voice. "My father was very ill. He needed constant attention."

"You use the past tense."

"My father died soon after."

"Sorry, I didn't mean to pry into your private sorrow."

"That's all right. You are the first to show any attention to me in the months I've been stranded out here."

"Surely, Doctor Faber. . . ."

"Bron is seldom here." I filed that away for future reference. He was seldom in either Cape Town or Johannesburg. Where did he spend his time, then?

"It must be very lonely for you."

"If Bron paid more attention to me, it would be bearable. As it is, well . . ." She shrugged and I knew then where Chinua had picked up the gesture. "This place is too dry. I am used to higher humidity, having lived below sea level near the Zuider Zee. The Netherlands is such a compact country, no waste space, so lush and pretty and colorful. Not like this." She glanced out over the veldt. The prairie-like expanse held only dust and exotic animals, not windmills and tulips and canals.

"Why not return to Europe? Or at least Johannesburg?" I asked. "There's no need to exile yourself out here if there's nothing to keep you occupied."

"Bron wants to get married soon. But the date is always a few weeks in the future. He says that Johannesburg is too violent a city, that Cape Town is too far away, that Pretoria is too provincial." She sighed. "Sometimes I think of leaving, going back to the Netherlands. But his work is so important I'd feel like a traitor leaving him."

"Which project is this? The insects? Or the disease prevention for the endangered species?"

"Both of those projects are completed. Bron talks of the plagues that will descend on all the cities due to the silly rules and regulations the South African ministers insist on enacting."

"What regulations are those?" I couldn't fathom her

meaning. Johannesburg was a modern, well-tended city, for all its social problems. The water supply in the city was adequate by any modern standard and sanitation didn't appear to be lacking. The *bantustans* might pose health problems, but hardly insurmountable ones, given the control the police demonstrated at every opportunity.

"I can't say. But Bron is sure that some horrible plague will soon destroy the major cities of South Africa."

In spite of the dry wind sucking away the moisture on my face, I shivered. Out here in the wilds of Africa, surrounded by beasts left over from the earliest eras of natural history, Bron Faber plotted to release a modern-day plague. And a better spot to perfect those plagues didn't exist in the world. The game preserve was patrolled regularly to keep out poachers. The vast areas remained uncharted and, if one of his genetically engineered diseases did get out of hand, there wouldn't be any real damage. No one but a few hyenas and wildebeest would notice.

This continent had been the cradle for humankind. It was now being turned into the incubation spot for mankind's grave.

"Where is Doctor Faber now?"

"Out there someplace," Alleen said dispiritedly. "His laboratory is hidden away so that snoops won't disturb him."

"That sounds like a good idea," I said. "He shouldn't be disturbed in the middle of a vital experiment. When do I get the chance to see his lab?"

"What?" She came out of her reverie. I had no idea where her mind had wandered, but it had left Africa entirely. Perhaps she thought of her dead father, her once-bright hope for marriage to Faber, the bustling city of Amsterdam. Wherever Alleen Kindt had been, she regretted returning to the here and now of the African veldt.

"Sitting around bores me. I like to be working. I want to get on with helping Doctor Faber."

"He left no instructions other than you'd be arriving today. I'm sorry, Herr Carter . . . ."

"Please, call me Nick."

Her smile was weak. "And I am Alleen. Now, Nick, Bron left no word on when or how you were to join him. Just become acquainted with the staff around here. Take Chinua with you and cruise about in the Land Rover. Get a feel for the animals, the terrain. Outside of that, I can offer no more advice." Again the shrug hinting at worlds of boredom she carried with her all the time.

"Would you accompany me on the trip?"

"Hardly, Herr Carter . . . Nick. I prefer to remain near the radio in case he calls."

She left the room, a defeated woman. It seemed a pity to waste such beauty on the barren glory of the African veldt. Alleen belonged at a jet-set party or a royal ball. She held herself as if money and pride had run through her family for generations and now she coped with the loss of both. It wouldn't surprise me to find that Faber had proposed marriage to tap into a very considerable family inheritance, then had to cope with the problem of a lovely young woman hanging around waiting for her wedding day.

Faber had a power over women I didn't understand. Erica der Klerk worshiped the ground he walked on. Alleen remained on, obviously long past the point where she knew that he'd never marry her. Even worse, she'd probably come to the conclusion that he'd been after her money.

The only hint this wasn't the case came in his refusal to allow her into the larger South African cities. He planned to unleash a plague of Biblical magnitude, of that there seemed little question, and he wanted Alleen safely distant. Or was his motive in this more pragmatic? Did he simply want her isolated so that she couldn't betray his plans before he was ready to spring it on an unsuspecting world?

Too many questions plagued me. I needed answers.

Chinua and I roared around scaring lions and monkeys all afternoon. I memorized the lay of the land, such as it was. A river nearby, a tributary of the Orange River, held more than its fair share of crocodiles and hippopotamuses. I didn't want to tangle with either for entirely different reasons. The crocs appeared to be somnolent and perpetually hungry. The hippos could step on me and do little more than wonder what the small lump had been under the back foot.

"It's so dusty around here," I remarked to Chinua. "Doesn't it ever rain?"

"Not much. Less than twenty inches a year. This year, it has rained less than ten."

"That qualifies the veldt as a desert." I observed.

His answer: a shrug.

I leaned back and let Chinua drive the Land Rover across every bump and pothole in South Africa. It was safe enough with a hard metal truck body around me but I didn't want to consider the potential for danger out on the plains, on foot, without weapons. Faber worked unmolested in such a place. In exchange for a few animals saved from diseases he might have caused in the first place, the South African government had given him free rein. What would the government ministers say if they found out they aided and abetted the research that had brought their country to its knees and frightened them all into submission?

Again, I cursed under my breath. There was no clear-cut, absolutely damning evidence against Faber. So he treated his fiancée badly? What if he was a fortune hunter? Those weren't nearly the heinous crimes Doctor DNA plotted.

"We must return soon," said Chinua. "Dinner is always at sunset." The cool wind whipping across the veldt told me that night approached. The day had been warm but the dark promised chilling cold. The daily shift in temperature seemed more like Colorado. Again the stereotype I'd had of Africa smashed headlong into reality.

"Turn back," I ordered. "Unless we're near Doctor Faber's lab. I'd like to see it as soon as possible."

"Never been to it," came the surprising answer.

"But how do you get supplies in? Aren't you the one responsible?"

"I work in the *kraal* and Faber takes care of the laboratory personally. He does not allow me to see it.''

I frowned. This struck me as bizarre behavior on Faber's part.

Alleen had never seen the lab, nor had the native serving as major-domo for the compound. It was almost as if this were a leper colony, a place where Faber kept unwanted visitors until they tired and left.

As we pulled into the compound, the odor of cooking meat greeted me. I inhaled deeply, savoring the aroma.

"*Braaivleis*," Chinua said laconically. Seeing my puzzled expression, he added, "Roasted meat, like American barbecue.''

The man hurried off to oversee supper while I wondered about him. No African native compared roast meat with barbecue. The idea forming in my head about this being a miniature prison for Faber's unwanted visitors solidifed into certainty. Whoever Chinua was, he wasn't "only" a Nigerian moved south.

We sat around a fire in the middle of the compound. I had visions of the American West and cowboys on a roundup. Only the lions roaring in the distance spoiled the image.

"Did you enjoy your trip today, Nick?" asked Alleen, sitting near me. She huddled in upon herself in such a fashion, she shut out most of the world, as if denying its existence.

"Interesting. I'd never seen so many animals I think of as zoo creatures roaming free. But the veldt's not a place I'd want to be." In the distance screeched a baboon. A lion's roar answered. The twilight provided prime hunting for the predators. Was Faber a predator? I hoped to make him my prey, if he turned out to be the man I sought.

"The novelty wears off in a few days."

"I hope to be in Doctor Faber's laboratory by then," I said.

"He radioed after you left with Chinua," she said, almost as if this were an afterthought.

"What did he have to say?"

"He'll be back at the end of the week. You're to remain here until he arrives.''

A leper colony, a holding area for those Faber wanted out of commission, that's where I was. That's where we all were, Alleen, Chinua, the others, myself. It wouldn't work. I didn't have the time to wait. Somehow, I'd have to find that laboratory and get the evidence I needed to prove or disprove that Faber was Doctor DNA.

"Good night, Nick," Alleen said, rising.

"You go to bed this early?" I asked, surprised. "It's hardly eight o'clock."

"There's little else to do." She vanished into the inky night. I retired to my own room soon after. Hidden in my suitcase was a small, powerful radio for reporting in to Hawk. I thought about using it, then decided I had nothing to report.

That was a lucky break for me. Moving through the night came a ghostlike figure. My room didn't have an electric light. I hadn't bothered to light the tiny propane lantern on the bedside table. Wilhelmina slipped easily into my hand as the door to my room opened with tiny, barely audible squeaks. The door closed and the dark figure moved slowly toward me.

"Nick," came Alleen's soft voice. "Are you awake?"

I sighed and put away Wilhelmina. Hugo followed, going under the bed.

"I'm here." I knew what she wanted. I wasn't going to turn her down. A warm body slid beside me on the bed. Her filmy peignoir vanished as if it had been nothing more than mist surrounding her supple, luscious body. My guess about her figure had been correct. She was beautifully proportioned. I knew. My hands told me what my eyes didn't see.

"Make love to me. Please. I need a man so badly. I'm so lonely!"

I silenced her with a kiss. We rolled over on the bed. She ended up on top. Her fingers ripped open my shirt. Buttons went flying around the room, banging onto the floor. Her cool, moist lips kissed my chest as she worked on my belt and trousers. All the time she undressed me, I caressed her magnificent breasts.

Those mounds of succulent flesh pulsed with life. I couldn't believe Faber was so stupid that he alienated such a lovely, loving woman. His loss was my gain.

I was hard by the time she got my pants pulled free of my ankles. I remained under her, on my back. Straddling my waist, the dark-haired woman moved so that her crotch was above mine. I felt the heat boiling from her interior. She lowered herself until moist nether lips lewdly kissed my manhood.

"Oh, it's been so long. I've been going out of my mind, Nick."

I put my hands on her hips and pulled her down. As her body sank, I shoved upward. We came together in a wet rush. Alleen rotated her hips, stirring my shaft around inside her like a spoon in a mixing bowl. I ran my hands over her hips, then up under her breasts to guide her in the motion I wanted most.

She ignored my promptings. Her carnal desires were too great for subtle pressures. She rose and fell, my erection entering and leaving her hot berth. Alleen speeded up, her hips moving in a sensuous circle even as she worked up and down.

Her passions reached the breaking point long before mine did. But that was all right. She had a lot of energy. Her lovemaking took on a frenzied air, as if she had been a virgin all her life and had suddenly discovered the wonders of sex. She seemed insatiable. For what seemed a blissful eternity, we moved, the divine friction burning away at our genitals.

When I no longer withstood her soft aggressions and wilted, she tried to keep on. Finally admitting defeat, she collapsed full length on my chest.

"It's been a long time for you, hasn't it?" I asked.

"Years. Centuries. I lost count. If only Bron didn't leave me to go out and play with his damn test tubes."

"He's a fool," I said.

"No, Bron's not a fool," she said. "He's driven. He has to accomplish something—and I can't help him achieve it. I wish I could. For him I'd do anything."

It got tedious listening to Faber's women tell me all about how much they lusted after him. But up to this point wasn't bad, not bad at all. Alleen left me in the middle of the night, the edge taken off her frustrated desires.

I felt cold and cynical but knew I could use those frustrations to my benefit. I'd have to do so to complete my mission.

So how did I differ from Bron Faber? I didn't want to think about the philosophical turnings of that question. I fought to prevent death and destruction and human suffering.

That had to be answer enough for me.

CHAPTER SEVEN

The next day, things in the *kraal* were tense. The way Alleen treated me, I might as well have had every disease her future husband had concocted in his laboratory. Chinua stared at me with a strange mixture of curiosity and aloofness, as if he wondered about me in the same way the public wonders what goes through a condemned man's head seconds before the switch is pulled.

I stopped Chinua and asked.

"It is nothing," he replied. "I have no animosity toward you."

"Something's happened. What?" I felt the way he drew back slightly. Body language speaks louder than words. I'd become an outcast. Finding out why meant the difference between life and death.

"You know what has happened," he said. "How you spend the night is your own business. When you spend it with Faber's wife-to-be, that is *his* business."

''And how did Faber find that out so damned fast? A jungle drum communication?''

''Gossip always spreads quickly in Africa,'' he said. The man turned and walked off without another word. He hadn't been hostile. If anything, after discounting the cool way he treated me, he had actually warned me of the danger. Chinua wasn't the one informing Faber of Alleen's and my indiscretion; if anything, Chinua had told me it was another of those in the compound. Who didn't really matter. I was in hot water over last night.

Sitting on the *stoep* and staring out over the veldt, I tried to formulate new plans. Action forced itself on me, yet all I could do was sit and wait. Going over my options didn't improve my outlook. Ministers were dying from Doctor DNA's diabolical diseases. The shipments of the extorted strategic materials continued unabated, going from Cape Town to some unknown port, probably in Namibia. The SWAPO guerrillas were tied into the unloading and reshipping, but to what extent? I didn't know. This was something I'd pieced together from Sam Uwanabe's comments.

And Bron Faber.

He was an even bigger enigma. Uwanabe mentioned him favorably as aiding the SWAPO wounded. He sold marijuana to street gangs in Johannesburg. His Cape Town office told of extensive overseas shipping. He had the facilities and the privacy to do any sort of DNA research he wanted—and without anyone being the wiser. He had some attraction for women I didn't understand. And I'd made love to both his nurse in Johannesburg and his fiancée here.

Faber's communications network operated at the speed of light, if he had really found out about Alleen and me. But none of this proved he was Doctor DNA, the man with the magical box that directed the disease-laden tsetse fly to its human target.

As I gazed out over the veldt, hardly seeing any of it, a dust cloud rose in the west. It grew until I heard the rumble of heavy trucks. A small caravan plowed through the dry roads toward the *kraal*. I had the gut-level feeling that the confrontation between Faber and me was approaching quickly. I went into my sleeping quarters and hastily donned both Wilhelmina and Hugo. "Be prepared" isn't only the Boy Scouts' motto. It's kept me alive over the years.

By the time I went back out on the porch, the lead truck had ground to a halt. Bron Faber bailed out of the passenger side. Natives climbed down from the back of the truck more slowly. I noted they all carried spears. None had a firearm of any sort. Faber almost ran to the main part of the compound and slammed through the door. I waited a few minutes, then went over.

"Is it true?" blared Faber at Alleen. The dark-haired woman cried so much that the dust on her cheeks had turned to mud. The way he intimidated her didn't sit well with me.

"Hello, Doctor Faber," I said as pleasantly as I could. "Glad to see you. Hope to get to working on your project soon."

"*You,*" he said, spinning and facing me. I thought lightning bolts would sear from his eyes.

"Yes?" I said mildly.

"You forced yourself on my fiancée. You raped her!"

"Hardly, Doctor. I want a job. I wouldn't do th—" He took two quick steps toward me and swung. Various possible actions flashed through my mind. I evaluated and discarded most of them. If I let him hit me, he'd do it again. If I decked him, he'd go for the pistol holstered at his side.

My hand blocked his blow, turning it aside harmlessly. He tried another punch. I blocked it, too. When I made no move to strike back, Faber retreated. My eyes fixed on his in a staring match. I felt the man tensing, ready to draw his pistol. My right arm twitched slightly in anticipation of such a move. Before his hand could touch the butt of his gun, Hugo would drink his blood. But I didn't have to pull my stiletto. Faber relaxed and backed off.

"You bastard," he said in a murderously low tone. "I hire you to help me and you rape my fiancée."

"No, Bron, it wasn't like that. I . . ."

"Shut up," he snapped. He shoved the woman down into a chair. I noted that he did it with one eye on me, as if seeing how far he could push me. When I didn't move he went to Alleen, grabbed her hair, and pulled her face up to look into his. "You bitch. Tell me the truth. He forced himself on you, didn't he? *Didn't he?*"

"Who gave you this bag of lies?" I demanded, my voice rising to pull his attention from Alleen. "Someone has told you things that just aren't true, Doctor Faber." My tone softened a little. I remained alert to a possible attack from him. I didn't miss the way the Bantus who'd come into the compound on the truck edged into the room, either. Four were behind me, two behind Faber. He had a small army inside the room, even if they were armed only with spears and knives.

"Who told me that you've been with my woman doesn't matter. It's true. I know it."

"Surely, a man of your stature can be forgiving. After all," I said, "aren't you affectionately known as Doctor DNA to the natives?"

"I thought so," he said. "You're no paramedic. You're a spy. You've been sent by *them!*"

"Why do you say that, Faber?" I had the proof I needed now. He hadn't denied it nor had he seemed too surprised when I called him Doctor DNA. My job still had a lot of details to be filled in. Where was his damned lab? If I destroyed it, would this destroy all his mutated diseases?

"A spy," he said firmly. "An American spy. CIA, probably. I thought you might be. You're trying to stop me from unifying all of South Africa. I can rule, but those fools in Cape Town and Pretoria stand in my way. Not for long. They're weakening. Soon they will abdicate and allow me to rule!"

"Rule? You sound like a king. King Bron the First, is that the way it's going to be?"

"All of Africa will be mine one day. I have the power. I will use it."

I'd touched on his megalomania and set off a diatribe. I hadn't thought his ambitions would stop with South Africa. With power such as that wielded by anyone able to direct virulent disease, nowhere in the world was safe. Even inside the Arctic Circle mosquitoes hatch. It wasn't that much of a jump from tsetse fly to mosquito—I had no idea what Faber worked on in his hidden laboratory. His tsetse fly might survive even in the arctic cold; it certainly thrived in tropical heat.

"Not even those Cuban stooges can halt my progress," he continued raving. "They might try. They'll fail because I control the most potent weapon in the world. Nothing can stop disease. And I'm the master of all diseases!"

"Bron, please," cried Alleen. He shoved her away.

I acted. As soon as he realized what he'd said, my death would be ordered. Whether or not he really thought I was a CIA agent, he'd have to get rid of me. It wouldn't do having a paramedic going around South Africa mouthing off about a man able to control the course of diseases.

The Bantus between me and the door stood with spears lowered. I knew getting past them was impossible. The four behind me were more at ease. They thought they had safety in numbers. I proved them wrong. A long, looping kick broke one's kneecap. He collapsed into a pile on the floor, moaning and writhing in pain. I took the next one's spear away from him with a sudden twist. The butt end smashed into his belly, doubling him up. A quick slash of the spear point took out the third. By this time the fourth moved. I dodged past his spear and rammed the shaft of my spear into his throat. Cartilage broke and pink froth spewed from his gaping mouth. His eyes rolled up and I knew I'd killed him. I turned, threw the spear at Faber, then dived out the window.

I hit the dust and rolled, coming to my feet. The trucks were ringed by a dozen more Bantus, all leaning on their spears and passing around a joint. The dope dulled their senses but not enough to allow me to get into one of the trucks and drive. The sounds of confusion inside the room behind me died down; pursuit was imminent.

I lit out running as fast as I could. Coming to a low ravine, I dropped into it and slowed my pace to an easy jog. At this pace I could do twenty miles without stopping. I wondered if that would be necessary before I eluded Faber.

The roaring noise of the truck engines turning over rumbled down the ravine. As long as I stayed in the deep cut, they couldn't spot me and their trucks would be useless. But the going got rough quickly. Roots tripped me and the debris proved treacherous. A spot that looked solid turned out to cover a sinkhole and a small brown rock wiggled away, hissing and complaining in a loud snake protest.

I kept going. I had to. If Faber caught me now, the lions would feed well tonight. And even if he didn't catch me, they might. This was the middle of the Kruger Game Preserve, miles from another human outpost. In the wild, the animals ruled supreme, all hunting for their meals. I wasn't a pushover target, but stopping to fend off the King of Beasts only set me up for Faber and his Bantu warriors.

I kept pounding away, slipping occasionally but making good time. When I found the tributary to the Orange River, I slowed and caught my breath. The river hadn't changed since my earlier visit. Crocodiles swam idly, barely making ripples in the scummy, sluggish flow. Hippos and an occasional rhinoceros frolicked in the shallows, covering themselves in mud. From further away I heard the trumpeting of a bull elephant—and the coughing of a truck engine.

There were few places to hide. This was a flood plain, washed clean every time it rained. Going back into the ravine hardly seemed a good idea. Why backtrack? I was sure that Bantus trailed me on foot. I'd run into them. Going out across the veldt looked even less promising as a way to continued survival. Faber's eyesight was good; one clear shot from a high-powered rifle would take me out of the game. That left the river, with its muddy, murky water.

When the truck rattled into view, I dived. Hitting the water at a shallow angle, I didn't cause too many new ripples to form. I swam along, blind from the mud, hoping I headed directly away from any hungry croc's fang-laden mouth. When my outstretched hand touched a slimy reed, I surfaced. A small clump of waterplants near the shoreline provided a small amount of cover. Peering out, I spotted Faber atop a truck, a heavy rifle in his hands.

While I might have been mistaken, I think he gripped a .610 Nitro Express rifle—an elephant gun. The passage of the bullet near my head would kill me; he didn't even need to hit me with that cannon. The heavy-caliber bullet kills from hydraulic shock and air is as much a fluid according to physics as is the blood in an elephant's arteries.

I winced as a leech decided to sample my leg. Then another and another. Hugo came into my right hand. I stabbed out, spearing two of the offending bloodsuckers. A rush in the water alerted me to incoming crocodiles scenting the fresh blood. I found myself caught between a rock and a hard place. If I stayed in the water, I'd make a hungry croc very happy. On the other hand, if I left my sanctuary Faber would spot me.

Taking my chances with the crocodile seemed less risky to me. I saw a thick, loglike reptilian head peering up out of the water, membrane slipping over the cold yellow eyes. Then the beast submerged. It made its death run.

I timed my leap perfectly. As it went for my legs, I surged up and out of the water and onto its back. Being in the shallows saved me. It twisted its seventeen-foot length with more agility than I'd thought possible for such a large beast. I hung on for dear life. I locked my legs around its leathery body and managed to get my left hand around its snout. I wanted to find out firsthand if the old tales about the muscles on a croc's jaws were right or not.

If they were, it'd take very little pressure to hold the jaws shut. If the tales were wrong, I would find out the hard way.

I trusted my instinct about the story being true. It was. My left hand easily held the crocodile's jaws shut while I maintained my position on the twisting, thrashing beast with my right hand and legs.

"Careful now," I said softly to my unwilling steed. "No sudden moves."

I heard Bantus muttering nearby on the shore. They didn't come to investigate the churning in the water. If I'd succumbed to a watery death, fine. If I hadn't, they didn't want to tangle with me. Faber's truck rumbled on, away from where I clung to my precarious perch. The croc eventually got off the muddy strip and into the water again. This time he unwillingly carried a passenger: me.

I maneuvered my living boat upriver, staying as close to the shore as possible. When I thought I'd outpaced the Bantus and left Faber way behind, I reached across the croc's back with my right hand, jabbed Hugo in far enough to draw blood and a reaction. As the beast snapped to the left, I kicked free and went right. Mud sucked at my feet as I found the shallows—and right behind came the croc, looking for revenge and an easy meal.

He was damn near as fast on land as I was, and I had a big incentive to move at top speed. I got up into a stand of trees and shinnied aloft. The croc glared at me with those baleful yellow eyes right out of hell, then flipped his ponderously powerful tail and returned to the river in search of easier prey.

I clung to that tree for almost an hour before my strength returned and I got all the blood leeches scraped off my legs and body.

After checking and cleaning Wilhelmina, I was ready for my assault on Faber's compound. No one ever accused me of being predictable. That's what has kept me alive so long. I did an infiltration sneak back along the ravine I'd used to get away from his *kraal* to find a hidden position less than fifty yards from the main building.

I saw Faber and Alleen arguing, but nothing like they had before. It sounded as if she'd actually forgiven him all sins. Alleen was a sensible enough woman. Why did she fawn all over Faber? Surely, she didn't entertain the same mad hopes he did about conquering the world. I'd talked with her enough to know that her dreams were more modest. A home, a family, happiness—and tranquility.

I melted back into shadow when one of Faber's Bantu guards glided by. The man moved well. I'd had very little warning of his approach. And whatever it was that alerted him of my presence couldn't have been very significant. He stopped and held up his head, as if listening. My first thought was that he scented me; in the jungle any European or American would have a different odor.

Whatever his clue, I didn't allow him to use it. My knife found his throat before he uttered a single cry. I dragged the dead man into the copse with me. Staying here didn't seem too wise anymore. I cleaned Hugo's blade in the dusty earth, then made my way toward the compound buildings. I made the sneak with my usual expertise—and it wasn't good enough.

I'd alerted the hunting-wise Bantus, and two of them pinpointed my location and homed in on me. Struggling on my belly along the airspace under the building, I knew only seconds remained before a fullscale outcry was raised.

Pushing up the floor boarding above me, I wiggled into the room. A tiny gasp sounded and a light flickered. I'd come up inside Alleen's bedroom.

"Nick!" she said, then lowered her voice. "He told me you'd died. An accident in the river."

"Faber's out to kill me, Alleen. You know that. His Bantus are after me right now. They're trained hunters. Their senses are too acute for me to elude them for long."

A banging on the door startled the dark-haired woman. She sat up fully in bed, her pale yellow peignoir falling open to expose those tempting, firm breasts.

"Who is it?" she demanded, her voice on the point of breaking with strain.

"Look for fugitive," came the heavily accented voice of one of the Bantus. "He's inside."

"I'm trying to sleep. Go away and leave me alone."

I dropped the flooring and rolled under her bed. Suitcases

and other boxes competed for room here, but I pushed my way through them to burrow into the middle. Alleen's weight caused the bed to sag down until the springs rubbed into my body. When I heard the door crash open, I drew my Luger. A few bullets wouldn't solve my problem but it might buy precious seconds to figure out some new escape plan.

"Get out!" screeched Alleen.

"Search the room," came a cold command. Naked feet with soles harder than any leather pounded toward the bed. From my vantage point, I saw only from the ankles on down. Four of them. Shooting now only signed my death warrant. I held off. For a few seconds.

Fate worked in my favor. A loud voice bellowed, "What are you doing in my fiancée's room?" Faber had noted the disturbance and had come to investigate. "Get out. How dare you intrude when she's dressed like that!"

I had to smile. Alleen ranked high on the beauty scale, no matter what culture. Faber was livid over anyone seeing his would-be bride more naked than dressed. And, perhaps, his upbringing in the Union made it all the worse when the eyes doing the ogling belonged to male natives.

"Doctor Faber, Doctor Faber!" came Chinua's voice. "The Angolans!"

"Damn," I heard Faber grumble, then louder, "Out, all of you get the hell out of here!" Footsteps vanished amid the roar of voices and intermittent rifle fire. I wiggled free from under the bed, Wilhelmina in hand.

"Nick, you're safe," cried Alleen. "I worried that he would . . . oh, what are we going to do?"

"Are the Angolans attacking? Inside South Africa?" It hardly seemed possible, yet South African troops had boldly raided deep into Angola last year. This might be a retaliatory raid, but it didn't seem likely. The middle of an eight thousand square mile game preserve is hardly vital territory. Whatever the attacking Angolans wanted, it was *here* and it was Faber's.

"Bron warned that they might. He . . . he's been doing

some experiments inside Angola. He said the Cuban-trained troops there didn't like it.''

"I can imagine. What sort of experiments? Did he say?'' I guessed pretty quickly what those tests might have been. I envisioned hundreds of guerrillas dying from creepy diseases that rotted the flesh from their bones, burnt out their internal thermometers with impossibly high temperatures, caused their innards to leak blood until the poor victim choked and drowned in his own juices. Yeah, I guessed why the Angolans were here.

"He never said. But their government ordered him from the country.''

I went to the window and peered out. The Angolans infiltrated well. At least a hundred of them surrounded the compound. Faber had fewer than twenty Bantus, and they weren't armed with anything more modern than a steel-tipped spear. Guerrillas don't much care about excuses when they attack. That Alleen and I were inside when they attacked would be enough reason to kill us, along with Faber and his native allies. I checked Wilhelmina. A shell rested snugly in the chamber.

"Watch them crawl,'' I heard Faber yell. "Watch them die!'' The laugh that echoed across the compound chilled me. There wasn't a trace of sanity in it. Bron Faber had gone off the deep end if he figured he could personally kill a hundred armed, Cuban-trained Angolan guerrillas.

Yet that's exactly what he did.

First came the electronic humming. Then sounded the whir of wings. A tsetse fly as large as my hand buzzed past the window. I came within a split-second of sending a bullet into it; it was too large to miss. But the tsetse fly intently drove into the darkness, singleminded in its determination to infect the guerrillas with whatever disease Faber had given it to carry.

Screams from the bush surrounding the compound became more frequent. The rifle fire came sporadically, then ceased. The only sounds from outside the *kraal* were agonized

moans. Some of the guerrillas turned their rifles on one
another—mercy killing. I watched as a camouflage-suited
guerrilla stumbled onto the porch not ten feet from me. His
face, normally black, had turned ashen. He ripped at his flesh
as if it had become infested with a billion fire ants. Only
terror and pain registered in his expression.

Walking dead. He was dead but his heart still pumped.
Dangerous bacteria chewed away at his guts and lungs and
brain, but he still lived and felt the agony of the disease.

I shot him through the head. Never have I seen a man's
face turn so peaceful knowing that swift death had taken him.

"God, Nick, what did Bron do to them? They . . . they're
all infected with something."

"One of his diseases. Even faster acting than the others
I've seen. It takes almost ten minutes for his genetically
mutated yellow fever to kill. Whatever this is kills in less than
a minute."

"Bron is doing this?" she said in a strangled voice.

"Look." I forced her to the window and held her head so
she couldn't turn away. Faber gleefully twisted the dials on
his electronic unit. One of the Bantus held a long probe—the
magnetic homing device that pointed out the victims for the
tsetse flies. A particularly large tsetse fly hummed around in
the air in front of the man. Faber grabbed the device form the
native's hand, then turned and pointed it at an Angolan
weakly attempting to crawl away. Like an arrow the tsetse fly
flew straight to the man. The image of a vulture-finding
carrion flashed through my mind as the fly landed in the
middle of the man's back. I watched helplessly as genetically
altered mandibles ripped through the thick shirt and bare
flesh.

The fly lanced out with its proboscis. The man arched
backward, his arms reaching up as if to implore an uncaring
god for mercy. Then the man's flesh seemed to churn and
ripple before it began flaking off in giant, grisly hunks.

Alleen made weak retching noises. I put my arm around
her and tried to stop the quaking I felt. Tending to her needs

came hard. Seeing such horrible misuse of science sickened me more than I cared to admit.

"Let's get the hell out of here. We might be able to get a truck and find the park ranger."

"No, Nick," she sniffled. "I can't leave. I can't leave him. Bron needs me."

"Needs you?" I yelled, both surprised and shocked. "The man's a butcher. You saw what he did out there. He's the one who mutated those flies. He's the one who's spent a lifetime working on new and more virulent diseases. How can you say he needs you?"

"I've got to try and stop him. It's the only way." The tremor had left her body. She firmed up and backed away. I saw that no amount of arguing would sway her, and there wasn't time enough for me to even try. When the bloodlust died down and Faber began thinking again, he'd remember the dead Bantu guard found before the Angolans arrived. He'd remember chasing out his men from Alleen's bedroom. He'd remember me.

"Stay here," she said. "I won't be long."

I didn't get a chance to argue with her. She picked up a thin robe, flung it around her shoulders and marched out into the middle of the carnage like some Valkyrie descending from Valhalla to pick up the valiant dead. She walked, straight to Faber, head held high, her step firm and confident.

I crouched down and pressed my ear against the wall. I heard what went on between them.

"Bron, you're responsible for all this, aren't you?"

"Alleen!" he cried. Another whoop of joy, then a loud, almost demented laugh. "Yes, this is my doing! Isn't it wonderful? I stopped an entire company of Angolans. In minutes I stopped them. They are all dead, dead, dead!"

"You did it with your diseases, didn't you?" Her voice trembled a little now. I fingered my Luger, wondering if I could get a clear shot at the man. Peering up over the window ledge, I saw it wasn't possible. Alleen stood between me and my target.

"Of course I did," he said, calming. "I've gotten twenty-five million in tribute from the South African government already. The Angolans will soon recognize me as their leader. And then, then I shall become King of South Africa!"

"King?"

"And you'll be my queen." He turned and stared out over the dark veldt. "It won't end here. The rest of Africa will fall. Or perhaps I'll let it rot. With the mineral wealth of southern Africa to finance me, perhaps I'll skip over to the United States or Europe. Yes, Europe. You shall be Queen of Europe, my dear. Queen Alleen!"

"I don't want to be queen," the dark-haired woman said. "I just want you."

Faber didn't hear. He rattled on.

"Word will spread because of what's happened here tonight. The Angolans will tell their Cuban masters. The Kremlin will learn of me. Then I shall crush Mother Russia. The French tried and failed. The Germans died attempting to conquer that country. I, Bron Faber, will succeed! Me and my little allies."

"Bron."

He went to the electronic box and turned a dial. Loud humming filled the still night. He picked up the magnetic aiming device and held it lovingly in his arms, as if it were a baby.

"All I need to do is point. The flies do the rest. I select which vector they shall carry, then they go forth at my bidding and infect!"

I lined up Wilhelmina for a shot. The distance wasn't too great but the angle was wrong and I never had a clear view. But I had to try taking Faber out now. It might be the last chance anyone would ever have.

My finger tightened. A shot rang out. I hesitated. The Luger hadn't fired; someone else had shot Faber. The man crumbled, then began rolling on the ground. Whoever had shot him hadn't scored clean. I rose, thinking I might finish the job already begun, but Alleen got in the line of fire. I actually thought about shooting her, getting her out of the way, then emptying the clip into Faber. The rush of Bantus around their fallen leader put all those thoughts to an end. I sank back under cover and watched.

Faber struggled to a sitting position, the wand in his hand. He pointed it out into the night, probably in the direction of the unseen sniper. A horrid buzzing filled the air as a dozen of the mutated tsetse flies roared to the attack. Even if it was a communist dupe, I hoped he made it safely back to Angola. No one deserved to die the way Faber promised.

"I'll rule them all!" he ranted. The Bantus picked him up and carried him into the compound, into what had been my bedroom. I let out the breath I hadn't known I was holding, then slid to the floor, back against the wall.

Alleen came in. She was as pale as a ghost and her hands trembled visibly. I didn't have to ask her what she now thought about her precious Doctor Bron Faber, saviour of all humanity.

CHAPTER EIGHT

"He'll kill us all," she said in a choked voice. I'd wondered how long it would take Alleen to realize that Faber no longer had both oars in the water. "I saw it in his eyes. That's not the man I loved, that's not Bron. This one . . . he's crazy!"

"You're not telling me anything I don't already know," I said. "He tried to kill me earlier when I was on a ship making its way down the western coast. He sent one of his Bantus with that gadget of his. I caught the tsetse fly."

"But why would he want to kill you? I mean," she said, her eyes dropping and a hint of blush coming to her wan cheeks, "before last night?"

"He's obviously got good communication throughout southern Africa. My cover was blown almost immediately after I got to Rabat."

"Cover?"

I sighed. The entire story was going to have to be told sooner or later. It had to be edited, though.

"I work for the U.S. government."

"A spy!" she said, awe tingeing her voice.

"Something like that. I'm more in the enforcement line than in intelligence gathering." That translated to a fancy way of saying Killmaster.

"And you came to stop Bron."

"I came to stop someone called Doctor DNA. It turned out he and Bron Faber are one and the same."

"Nick!" she cried, gripping my arm. There wasn't any need for the warning. I'd already seen the Bantus returning to her quarters. They hadn't finished their search. This time I didn't think I could count on the Angolans to provide a handy diversion. All the guerrillas lay rotting out under the bright silver light of a freshly-risen moon. It cast an eerie pallor over the battleground. The corpses seemed to churn and move with pseudo-life. I knew it was the voracious African insects moving into the compound, despite Faber's genetically engineered inderdict against them.

In this country, food took priority over even the most frightful of dangers. If you didn't risk everything for a mouthful of food, there wasn't any other chance of surviving.

"There are three of them, Nick," she said, staring out the window. Alleen had frozen to the spot. The time had long passed when I should have made a run for it. But the big problem remained: run where?

The park rangers' headquarters lay a full forty miles down the road and, from what Chinua had said, none of the rangers might be there. They patrolled over a quarter of the eight thousand square mile preserve. In Jeeps, that took a long time. The chance of me making it to my radio ranked even lower on the scale of things to happen. Faber lay in my old quarters, probably just inches away from the radio that could bring in help from outside. Those were minor considerations, however. My mission remained incomplete. Faber lived and his laboratory out in the veldt hadn't been discovered yet.

And, as much as I hate to say it, I felt a responsibility for Alleen. She'd gotten herself into this, but if I could save her

I'd have to do it. I silently prayed that it didn't come down to a choice between saving her and finishing the mission.

That choice left her high, wide—and dead.

I spun and rolled so that I ended up under her bed again. This time I pulled down the sheet in such a fashion that the trio of Bantus entering the room wouldn't see me immediately. Wilhelmina was cocked and ready to take lives.

The door burst inward as the lead native kicked it open. I waited. Alleen acted as I'd thought she would. Backing away, a horrified expression on her face, she drew their attention. The other two crowded in behind the first. My finger tightened three times. Three bullets found their marks. The first native hardly knew he'd been hit before the last slug ripped through the air, on its way into the heart of the last.

I came out, shook Alleen hard, and harshly ordered, "Get dressed. We're getting out of here. They might not notice a couple of shots being fired, but when Faber doesn't see you beside him, he'll send more of his natives. Now, get dressed." I had to shake her again.

In other circumstances watching the lovely, dark-haired woman dress would have been pleasant. Now the clock dictated too much. She moved with maddening slowness. What seemed hours later, she stood completely outfitted for a long stay in the bush. The safari jacket she'd worn when I first saw her hung like a tent. She slumped and had that beaten, defeated posture that caused her to shrink in upon herself.

"Do you have a gun? A rifle? Shotgun? Anything?"

The tiny shake of her head sent her hair slithering down into her eyes. She brushed it back, hardly noticing she'd done so.

"If we steal a truck, can you get me to Faber's lab? The one out in the veldt?"

"I . . . I don't know where it is. Bron never took me there."

I cursed, then forced myself to remain calm.

"You know what direction it is. Surely he didn't try to hide

that. Which way did he always drive in when he left here?''
Alleen pointed in a vague westerly direction. I nodded. Faber
had come from that direction before this gruesome bloodbath
had started. I remembered sitting and seeing the dust clouds
kicked up by his trucks as they approached.

"Can we get away alive, Nick?"

"We can," I said firmly. "Trust me. I'm good at this."

For some reason that seemed to soothe her. I saw the
tenseness relieved in her facial muscles and the set of her
body became more confident. In a lot of situations, it pays to
be self-assured. I hoped that I could deliver now that I'd
promised her things would go great. I wasn't half as sure as
I'd sounded.

"The trucks. Some are leaving."

I looked out the window. Alleen was right. I wondered if
those three Bantus lying dead on the floor had been sent to
take the woman to Faber—or kill her. I watched as the natives
helped Faber out of the building and into the back of a truck.
It roared off, kicking up a cloud of dust. Two other trucks
remained.

It was now or never.

"Come on, Alleen. Run for all you're worth!" I jerked so
hard on her arm I thought I'd dislocated her shoulder. She
squawked in protest but I didn't let her think about what we
did.

The decisions had flashed through my mind in less than a
second. I could wait here and check to see if Faber had found
my radio in my quarters. If he had—and had destroyed
it—we'd be relatively safe for the moment. He obviously
intended to abandon this compound. If the radio worked,
reinforcements were only hours away.

I discarded that course of action almost instantly in favor of
running for the trailing truck. They were returning to Faber's
lab. I had a chance to destroy it and Faber. If they got too far
into the veldt, it might take weeks of searching to find them,
even knowing the general direction they'd taken.

The trucks had carried a full complement of natives when
they'd arrived. The Angolans had taken their toll, as I had.

The last truck pulled out, empty in back. Alleen pounded alongside me, her lungs gasping for air in the thick dust. That worked for us more than against us by cloaking our desperate bid to gain the tailgate.

I jumped, caught hold of the tailgate chain and pulled myself in. The truck sped up. I turned and found Alleen's hand the instant before a burst of speed would have left her in the center of the road. Heaving, I got her into the truck.

"Stay low," I said. The rattling of the truck covered any sounds we might make. All we had to worry about was the driver glancing into the rear-view mirror and spotting us. As long as we huddled against the front end of the compartment, there was little chance of being discovered. I held Alleen's hand tightly. She managed a weak smile.

In my head I went over the battle plan when we arrived at the hidden laboratory. Everything had to work perfectly the first time. I would never get a second chance. Faber still had a dozen natives with him. He might have that many more at the lab. While Erica der Klerk in Johannesburg had said Faber needed a new assistant, she'd first said he had already hired one. The newly opened position might have come from Faber's suspicions about me. He might have wanted me to stay where he could keep an eye on me—with Alleen, Chinua, and any others who might poke around too much.

So, I faced about twenty-five Bantus, Faber, and an assistant.

Wilhelmina's clip still held three rounds. I had another clip in my pocket. Hugo rested coolly against my right forearm. My gas bomb, Pierre, snuggled close to my groin. And I had one ally of questionable use: Alleen.

"Are you doing okay?" I asked.

"Fine, Nick."

"You're lying."

"Why did he have to do this to me?" she said. But there weren't any tears. She was all cried out. "I loved him. I . . . I guess I still love him, no matter what. But how could he do this to me?"

"He's been bitten by the worst bug of all—power. He used

to be a good man, the man you loved. Then he tasted power and became addicted. It's happened to stronger men.'' I lied through my teeth. The ones like Bron Faber were never good men. They always lusted after control over others. Alleen had been duped by him. The death of her father, the presence of Faber, that magical control he seemed to have over women, smooth talking and a cool manner—all had turned her confusion into love. He had used her. Eventually Alleen would realize this. If she lived long enough.

Right now I just wanted to ease her emotional pain.

''How long does it take to get to the laboratory?'' I asked, hoping the question would bring out information she didn't know she possessed.

''He's never back sooner than three days.''

I considered. Possibly eight or ten hours drive. The truck hit a pothole that must have gone all the way to the earth's core and tossed us together. We clung to one another like frightened children. The prospect of spending time this close to Alleen, under other circumstances, might have been delightful. As it was, we were caked with dust and developing bruises in places I didn't even realize could bruise.

''Bron said he wanted to make the world better for all mankind. His research made disease obsolete.''

I said nothing. Let her talk it out. After a while, the dark-haired woman ran down and contented herself with resting her head against my chest. It presented a poor pillow but neither of us complained.

The trip lasted a bone-jarring seven hours. By the time I heard the horns of the trucks ahead honking, I was tired, hungry, thirsty and almost comatose. Alleen presented a figure hardly better.

''Out. Now,'' I ordered. ''We've got to stay clear of the laboratory. They might have sentries on duty after the Angolan mess at the other compound.''

We dropped off. My legs buckled under me. They were stiff and bruised and barely straightened. I helped Alleen to her feet. Like a pair of aging cripples, we hobbled off for cover, lost in the perpetual dust cloud kicked up by the trucks. We blended in well with the terrain. Our clothes were completely covered in the brown grit and our faces looked like dirt masks with eye, nose, and mouth holes.

"There it is," I said after the trucks had stopped and the dust settled. A series of low buildings near a heavily wooded area housed the laboratory of Bron Faber, Doctor DNA.

I wiped off Wilhelmina's toggles and checked the slides to make sure they were free of grit, then prepared to make my assault.

I advanced on the laboratory just before dawn.

"Stay here," I told Alleen. From here on out, she'd only get in the way. The last thing in the world I wanted was someone stumbling along and alerting Faber's guards. I'd watched carefully and had the three sentry posts firmly in mind. The Bantus hadn't been trained properly. They left gaps in the defense.

After a brief recon, I decided that no one had attacked this lab before and they didn't expect anyone to do so now. With a little luck, I'd make it in, destroy the test tubes laden with disease, bacteria and virus, get rid of the tsetse flies—and remove Bron Faber. It seemed like a lot but I'd already gone through hell getting here.

I might even get a few answers to questions bothering me. How had Faber spotted me so fast on *The Easy Ride?* The Bantu put aboard the ship at Walvis Bay had been directed straight for me. They'd known I was an agent—but how? What made it even stranger was the lack of recognition on Faber's part when I'd applied for the job at his Johannesburg Medical Research Center. If he'd known of me on the ship, why hadn't he known me then? Or had he only been told an agent working against him was aboard *The Easy Ride?*

If so, that partially answered the question. He'd thought the Bantu had succeeded. There hadn't been any failures up to that point, so why expect one against a man masquerading as a sailor?

But how had he found out I'd been assigned in the first place?

If the rest of the mission went well, this might explain itself. Enough pieces to the puzzle often gave a bigger picture than anything imagined in more hectic times.

"Do I have to stay here, Nick?" she asked.

"It's going to get dangerous. If I make it, everything'll be fine. If I don't, try to get back to the compound." I explained about my radio and how to use it. I didn't bother telling her who would be on the receiving end of the message or what they'd do with her information. "They'll take care of Faber and make things work just fine for you."

"They'll kill him, won't they?"

"Not if I get to him first. Look, Alleen, I've been over this. Faber's a dangerous man, very dangerous. He's killed seven government ministers I know of with his genetically altered diseases. He's going to wreck the balance of peace and force us into war. The Soviets don't like being blackmailed any more than the U.S. does. And it's only a matter of time before the South Africans figure out he's one of their own and crack down on him."

"I know," she said in a soft voice. "Still . . ."

"Wait here. I don't know how long this will take. Possibly an hour. I intend to make it less, if I can." I kissed her on the forehead and took off into the bush.

Then I changed from Nick Carter, concerned man, into Nick Carter, Killmaster.

It's taken me years to perfect my infiltration techniques. I've studied with the best and learned from the best. From previous experience, I knew the Bantus had acute senses. They lived or died on their daily hunting skills; they were formidable opponents. But for all their empirical expertise, they didn't match the combination of the technical and theoretical I possessed.

I made my way through their defense perimeter without being detected. At the nearest building, I rose and peered inside. I'd hit it lucky. An empty office. A quick wiggle got me through the open window and into the room. I snaked across the floor to the desk and began going through it for the information I sought.

I'm no scientist but I do have enough education to know the real thing when I see it. The folders in the drawers told of Faber's experiments with the insects. He had discounted the mosquito because of his inability to genetically change its size. The tsetse fly proved a better subject for him. From one document, I noted that he'd developed one strain larger than a canary. I whistled long and low at that. It'd take a baseball bat to knock one of them out of the air.

Other information flowed when I pried open a file cabinet. The details of the disease experiments were excerpted. I ripped the important pages out of the notebooks and crammed them into my pockets. AXE scientists would be interested. The rest I hurried through and failed to find anything that set off the alarm bells in my head indicating importance.

Worst of all, I failed to find a detailed outline of Faber's plans. How did he select the ministers to die? What extortion demands had he made of them? Who were the connections for the metals shipments in Namibia? I found this odd because everything else had been so carefully written down.

I began spilling the papers onto the floor. When I had a nice pile, I flicked my cigarette lighter and ignited the corner farthest from the door. In a few seconds, I had a hearty fire roaring up toward the roof. Waiting a few seconds longer to make sure the blaze fed properly almost cost me my life.

One of the Bantu guards outside raised an alarm.

I sped out the door—into the arms of one of the natives.

He was as surprised as I was. I recovered first. Hugo slipped out and sank into the man's chest, the stiletto point angling up past the ribs and into the heart. He died without another sound. But the confrontation had taken precious seconds. The fire alarm brought others running from all over. They saw me.

"Kill him!" It was obvious they all wanted me very dead.

Spears whined past my head as I ducked and moved away.

They rushed. I turned, Hugo slashing one man's belly open. He cried out in pain and surprise and then turned and fell into the arms of the warriors behind him. This gave me enough time to make a frontal assault on the next building. I hoped it was the lab containing the living diseases and insects. One good fire would destroy all of it, just as the other fire I'd started burned Faber's records into ash.

"What's going on here?" demanded a man in the doorway. I barreled into him and knocked him over. But he moved well. Recovering, coming to his feet, he faced me.

"So, you're Faber's assistant," I said.

"Who are you?" he demanded. "What's happening here?"

The man I faced had bushy brown hair, graying slightly at the temples, and the beginnings of a spare tire around the middle. He had carried the yellow-fever-laden tsetse fly that had killed Dieter Karlik. This had to be Faber's assistant.

"Your death," I said, lunging. My knife slashed along the man's ribcage. I missed a clean kill and produced only a fountain of blood. If anything, a cut is virtually painless because of the clean severing of the nerves. In a while, though, the loss of blood would catch up with the man.

I didn't have time. The Bantus milled about, leaderless. Some wanted to put out the fire. Others wanted to find me. As a result of their indecision, neither got done. That wouldn't last long, though.

"You're Carter," the man grated from between clenched teeth. I attacked and missed him entirely this time. He danced back, one hand holding the wound and the other groping for something on a shelf. I stepped back, gauged the distance between us and started forward for the kill when he pulled down a wand.

"Die, Carter. See how the tsetse flies enjoy your flesh!"

He pointed one of the guidance sticks directly at me. It had to be a newer model than the others I'd seen. This required no camera case-sized power pack. Self-contained, it was hardly the thickness of my middle finger and about two feet long.

I acted instinctively. Hugo flashed out, turning over twice

in midair before burying itself to the hilt in the man's throat.
The wand fell to the floor and clattered away. I went for it
instead of my knife. The buzzing in the air alerted me to the
aerial danger confronting me.

The tsetse flies were immense. These weren't the canary-
sized ones I'd read about in Faber's papers, but they came
close. I recovered the wand and stared at it. I had no idea how
to turn it off. I started to smash it when the sound of the
natives outside made me change my course of action.

I pointed the wand at the doorway. The tsetse fly in the lead
raked mandibles across the first Bantu's throat. I watched in
horror as the flesh seemed to boil away from the man's bones
in a gray cascade. Killing is something I'm forced to do for
my country, but my weapons are more personal, cleaner.
Knife, gun, bare hands, those are what I know best.

This type of killing sickened me.

The flies poured from hidden compartments and swarmed
out into the group of now-terrified natives. I didn't worry
about them any more. They'd be off and into the bushes,
running for their lives. If I had any sense, I'd join them.

Instead, I poked around, seeking out Faber.

He wasn't in this lab. That left the third building, the one
most carefully hidden from aerial surveillance. Going out a
window, I made my way to the last lab building, keyed up
and ready to finish my mission. What I'd done to the Bantus
shouldn't have been done to any living creature, yet they'd
used that wand on others, too. In a way, they reaped what
they'd sown. Still, the real genius behind the genetically
altered insects and diseases remained at large.

Bron Faber had to die.

A bullet whined past the side of my head. I dodged, rolled,
and came up behind one of the trucks. Another bullet flat-
tened a tire. I crawled under the truck and studied the building. Two windows, one door on my side. At least one
window per side all around, I guessed. Another door on the
far side. I had no idea of the odds against me now. At least
one man with a rifle. I figured it was Faber.

Knowing I couldn't keep up a one-man siege very long, I

attacked. Straight on, feinting to one side, moving to the other, running, ducking, constantly moving. The bee's flight of angry bullets never found me. Panting, I crouched against the wall, the window just over my head. Wilhelmina rested comfortably in my hand.

"Let's compromise, Carter," came Faber's voice from inside. "I can kill you. But you're a brave man. You've shown great courage. Now show great wisdom. Join me. I can make you into a prince, a ruler, the wealthiest man on the continent!"

I sidled along the wall, heading for the second window. Faber was closer to the one I left and I had a chance to get behind him.

"Money? Do you want money, Carter? It's yours! Power? Ask! I'll give it to you."

I called out, "You wouldn't understand what I want, Faber."

"Women? You're quite a ladies' man. All the women you want, Carter. That's an easy one for me. Join me and you can have anything you want."

"Anything but self-respect."

"You're a fool!"

I twisted and vaulted into the room, coming to a crouch, Wilhelmina pointed. I hadn't counted on entering into a separate room. I'd mistakenly thought this building had been laid out like the others—one giant room inside. My gun covered one of the Bantus, not Faber. The scientist was in the next room.

"Don't even breathe," I said softly. The native raised his hands. But the widening of his eyes betrayed the fact that we weren't alone in the room. I sprang sideways, slamming hard into the wall. My Luger swept around and fired. The native sneaking up on me jerked, a bullet lodged in his brain.

The haft of a spear smashed into the back of my head. I fell, half-stunned, paralyzed and only weakly kicking. Through blurred vision I saw the steel-tipped spear rise, both of the man's hands on the shaft. This was going to be a quick, clean death.

And I was going to be the one dying. My muscles refused to move. I struggled and was rewarded only with the look of triumph on the Bantu's face.

The triumph changed into pain. The spear came forward but it missed by body. It sank an inch deep in the hardwood flooring. The native toppled over me. By this time, limited muscle control had returned. I pushed the man off and saw a knife protruding from his back. I shook off the last of the stunning blow and focused my eyes.

Chinua stood at the far side of the room, his face split into a wide smile.

"I did better with him than I did with Faber. My knife throwing has always been superior to my marksmanship with a rifle."

"Chinua? Why?" I asked. Wilhelmina appeared in my hand, as if by magic, even as I uttered the last question.

"No need for that, Carter. We're both on the same side," Chinua explained as he came to me. "Nasty bump. You've got a mild concussion. After I finish with Faber, you'll have to have that examined."

"What's your beef with him?"

"I said we're on the same side. Not the same team, perhaps, but we go after the same thing. I am Nigerian."

"And?"

"And I am a member of a select group empowered by the Organization of African States to . . . police our continent."

"You're a spy."

He laughed quietly. "Yes, I am that. We spotted one another too quickly. We are both in the business too long. It shows. Faber became suspicious of me and kept me with Alleen and others he distrusted. Not until you arrived did events move swiftly enough for me to act."

"That was a difficult shot. It was dark."

"I should not have missed Faber." Real wistfulness came to the man's voice. "It made the job much harder. I have had no chance at him until this moment."

"Then let's do it together."

Chinua smiled again. I didn't know about any undercover agents for the OAS, but it didn't come as a shock. Africa has produced some wild-eyed dictators with the potential for shaming Hitler when it comes to outrage. The more moderate states in the OAS might have decided that mere political pressure didn't alter the course of those dictators, so they'd gone to more covert practices.

Africa was becoming just like the civilized nations of the world. I wasn't sure if this was an improvement or not.

"In there," said Chinua. I stopped, took a steadying breath, then kicked the door open.

Neither Chinua nor I had a clean shot at Faber. He hunched down near the window. A table loaded with glassware blocked him from a quick bullet out of Wilhelmina's barrel or Chinua's flashing knife. Bron Faber jerked his rifle around and fired three quick shots in our direction. Glass went flying everywhere. I ducked and went right while Chinua moved left. I liked his style. He reacted in the proper way without being told.

Maybe he was right. Maybe we were a lot alike. Maybe we'd been in this business too long.

Faber let out a screech like a banshee, then stood and pumped a half dozen rounds into the bench on the opposite side of the room. I froze inside. Chinua had gone behind that bench. The high-powered rifle easily shot through the wood.

Chinua half-rose clutching his chest. Blood spurted out, indicating that an artery had been nicked. Not even shock would close it off before he bled to death.

"Drop it, Faber!" I cried. I braced my Luger against a table. The man filled my gunsights.

He turned and dropped the rifle, saying in an oddly small voice, "I'm out of bullets."

I saw red. AXE would have liked Faber alive to pick his brains but everything the scientist had done came crashing in on me then. He'd killed Chinua, probably one of the cleanest deaths in his crime spree. The suffering and the fear this lone man had caused couldn't be reckoned. Disease, horrible, awful disease that gnawed and tore at a man's guts. The dope he pushed to teen-agers in Johannesburg. The demoniacal glee he'd exhibited when he'd wiped out the Angolan guerrillas with his army of tsetse flies.

I stood and my finger tightened on the trigger. What ran through my brain was that I should get a medal for killing scum like Bron Faber. A body hurled toward me from my blind side. A petite hand slapped into my gunhand. The Luger fired. The heavy slug blew splinters off the window frame to the side of Faber's head. I found myself struggling with a wildcat.

I tossed her away. Alleen lay in a heap on the floor, sobbing, "I love him, I still love him. God protect me."

Outside an engine roared. I ran to the window and saw a truck barreling down the road until the cloaking dust blocked it from view. I'd be after him soon enough. I went to Chinua to see if I could do anything for him.

He lay in a pool of his own blood. His hand felt cold and barely twitched. His eyes opened and focused.

"D-don't be too harsh with her," he said in a whisper. "It is not her fault."

"She knows what a beast he is," I snapped.

"She cannot help it. No woman can."

"What do you mean?"

Chinua coughed. Blood dripped from the corners of his mouth. He winced but fought for a few extra seconds of life.

"Faber's first experiments. Aphrodisiac for Bantus. He has altered pheromones. Women find him irresistible because of his mutated pheromones."

That's the last he said. I laid Chinua's head down gently and stared at Alleen, who still sobbed. Things spun out of control around me. She had stopped me from killing Faber because the man smelled good. Sure, I knew there was more to it than that. Pheromones are tied strongly with sexual desire and Faber apparently controlled his through genetic engineering. It explained Erica der Klerk; it explained Alleen Kindt; it explained why the Bantus followed Faber initially.

"The bastard smells good," I raged. "That stinks!"

I left Alleen in the ruined laboratory and headed for the truck. This time Bron Faber would die.

CHAPTER NINE

When things fall apart, they go to hell all the way. I'd rushed out, the bloodlust still in me. If I'd found a working truck, I would've overtaken Faber within minutes and used my bare hands to strangle the life from his miserable carcass.

If, if, if.

None of the remaining trucks was operational. One had a flat tire. Another had taken several rifle bullets through the engine block. The one parked in front of the office had exploded from the fire I'd set, and a fourth, parked some distance away, refused to start. A quick look under the hood failed to reveal why.

Faber had gotten away and left me in the dust. He had driven off and I had no idea where he might be heading. Disgusted, I went back into the lab to search it more thoroughly. My luck wasn't holding up too well; now was the time to change it and find a working radio to call Hawk and report.

No radio. No live disease virus or bacteria. The tsetse fly-breeding area in the second building vanished as soon as sparks from the office fire jumped over and touched the thatch roof. I ranted and rampaged like a bull in a china shop trying to uncover the slightest of clues in the remaining lab.

Alleen still sniffed occasionally. She sat huddled on the floor, her back against a wall as if expecting me to strike her at any instant. For a moment I thought she deserved it, but I found I was as mad at myself as at her. Maybe even more so. For a few minutes before she'd entered the picture, I'd had a chance to take out Faber—and failed. Maybe no one could have done better.

But I'm not just anyone. I'm Nick Carter, Killmaster.

Ha.

"W-want me to help? I-if you tell me what you're l-looking for, I'll help." She stammered when I glared at her.

My mood softened. I recognized my own failings. She was a civilian. There was no cause for me to blame her if I had failed in my mission.

I sat beside her, my back against the wall as well. I took her trembling hand and squeezed it reassuringly.

"I'm sorry, Alleen. Sorry for getting you into this. What Chinua said changes things a lot. Faber's got more tricks up his sleeve than I realized."

"I . . . I never knew about the pheo—whatever," she said. "What was Chinua talking about?"

"Insects attract their mates through the use of airborne hormones. Pheromones. Faber probably worked with them at some time while developing his giant-sized bugs. He probably also realized the power he could wield over the Bantus if he mutated human pheromones into aphrodisiacs."

"Humans have them, too?"

"All animals have them. Why do women use perfume, men aftershave and cologne? It's our way of replacing the natural pheromones we wash off."

"And this is what attracted me to Bron? I don't believe it."

"It helped. The man's smooth. Any extra chemical help

only added to his appeal. Remember Erica der Klerk and her
fanatical attraction to him?''

"Yes," she said sullenly. "The slut's probably been to
bed with him more than I have."

"She's never gone to bed with him. Something about the
pheromones he uses brings out her fantasies. Who can say
what's been triggered in her head? This is a brand-new
field."

"A perfume company would pay a lot for his secret," she
said, as if slowly realizing the possibilities.

"I'd pay a lot to be alone with him for five seconds. Three
seconds." It wouldn't take me longer than that to kill him.

"Nick, I'm sorry. Even after you explained all this to me,
I'm sorry." She cried again. I put my arm around her and
comforted her the best I could. I needed her calm so she'd
remember the little things the man had said to her.

"Where do you think he's headed now?" I asked softly.

"I don't know. I . . . just . . . don't . . . know!''

I saw it wouldn't do any good pursuing the matter. She was
too shaken to give coherent answers. We went outside where
I got to work changing the bullet-punctured tire on the truck
nearest the lab. For two men it's hard work. For one it was
almost impossible. Alleen tried to help but she got in the way
more than she aided. Finally, I got the massive tire replaced
and the engine turned over.

But where to go?

I turned off the engine and decided that tracking Faber in
the dust out on the veldt bordered on the impossible. I had no
idea which direction he'd taken. Since I'd been marooned
here for almost three hours, the headstart he had was insurmountable.

"Nick," called Alleen, coming from the lab. "I've
searched the place looking for a radio. I . . . I thought he
might have one hidden. There's nothing. I'm *so* sorry." She
burst into tears again.

"Come on, let's get away from here. First, get some
blankets and food and put them in the back of the truck.'' She

did as I told her, trying to get a hold of herself while she packed the truck. I torched the laboratory. We drove a half mile into the veldt and looked back. The flames lashed high above the sheltering trees. I hoped that the dry grass of the veldt wouldn't catch fire. Such an inferno would sweep across a quarter of South Africa. Still, the flames purified the festering breeding ground for the mutated tsetse flies.

Risking conflagration for such a worthwhile end seemed justified to me.

"You rest in the back. I'll drive us back to the compound. Maybe my radio's still there and workable. Maybe Faber's headed there, himself." I doubted that. When he'd abandoned the *kraal* it was for good. Whichever way he ran now, it wouldn't be to an old haunt.

At least, not to an old haunt I knew anything about.

I turned to look at Alleen to make sure she was safely in back of the truck. She had finally calmed down, but she hadn't budged from the front seat. She seemed to sit there lost in thought.

"What are you thinking about?" I asked, gently.

"Namibia," she sighed.

"Why Namibia?" I asked, suddenly alert. The strangeness of her answer took me by storm.

"I don't know," she said, unaware of the change in my attitude. "It just sort of came into my head, that's all. Why?"

"What about Namibia?" I repeated.

She turned and stared at me.

"Was it something Faber said? Something he did? Had you overheard a conversation where Namibia was mentioned?"

"I might have. I don't know. I've never been there. Except . . ."

"Yes?"

"Maybe it was something Bron said. He had shipping interests in Namibia. Walvis Bay and Windhoek."

"Windhoek?"

"Another port in Namibia, I suppose. I don't know."

"That's the capital. And it's not a seaport. It's some miles inland. Faber shipped through his Cape Town office. I think he shipped the strategic metals he extorted into Namibia where the SWAPO guerrillas unloaded them. He moved the metals to another port and shipped to European smelters."

"SWAPO," she said, as if remembering a name that had tormented her memory for long hours. "He *did* mention SWAPO. And Windhoek. They were mentioned together. I overheard him talking long-distance to Cape Town. He was going to meet someone in SWAPO in Windhoek!"

"Did he have another laboratory in Namibia?"

"What? I don't know. Why should he? He had the one here." She glanced out the window of the truck. The fire still burned but the flames had dropped below tree level now. Only a pillar of thick, oily smoke twisted upward to mar the clear air over the veldt.

"Faber's not the kind of man to put all his eggs in one basket. I'm betting he had his little research empire scattered throughout all of southern Africa. This was his breeding ground for the tsetse flies. I found no evidence of his disease research here, not the physical presence." I instinctively checked my pockets. The papers detailing the plasmid gene splicing were still safely tucked away. "I think he carried on that research somewhere else."

"In Namibia!"

"Yeah," I said, warming to the topic. "Namibia is a country in a state of internal conflict. Not quite civil war, but close. He made a deal with the SWAPO guerrillas opposing the South-Africa-supported DTA. His money—coupled with the potential for threatening the government with disease—kept the officials off his neck. He shipped the metals into Namibia, got payment there and kept his laboratory nearby. In Windhoek."

"Would he put his lab in the capital?" Alleen asked.

"Maybe not in the capital, but Namibia is like South Africa. There's a lot of open country."

I didn't continue my line of reasoning out loud. The Bantu

who'd tried to kill me had already been in Walvis Bay. If
Faber's headquarters was nearby, it explained much. A native didn't have the freedom to travel in Namibia any more
than he did in South Africa. Crossing the border between the
two countries was next to impossible without a ton of paperwork. The almost-starving native on board *The Easy Ride*
hadn't come from too far off. Not more than a few miles.

I'd never been in the country between Windhoek and
Walvis Bay, but it seemed the best place to start.

"Come on, Alleen," I said, taking her by the hand and
dragging her out into the bright sunlight. "Let's make sure
this old bus has enough gas to get us across Africa. We're
going to Namibia."

Some things are easier said than done. While we had
enough gasoline scavenged from the other trucks, I had no
real idea where to go. I had no maps and driving straight as an
arrow into the west posed even more problems. Another
country got in the way. Still, the entire trip amounted to only
eight hundred miles or so. A hard day's drive on good
pavement and no cops worrying about speed limits, but two
or even three over the veldt.

We made good time, though. I maintained a pretty constant forty, sometimes pushing it up to sixty. The truck
complained bitterly at this speed so I dropped back now and
then to keep it happy. Once out of the Kruger Game Preserve
we hit road, but I hesitated about staying on the paved track.
South Africa was a police state. We didn't have the papers to
be traveling, nor did I have a good feel for the kind of
explanation it would take to get us out of jail if word of the
massacre out in the veldt reached the authorities.

So, I had to choose. I decided to hell with the police, stay
on the road.

And almost immediately, we ran into a police roadblock.

"What do we do now, Nick? Shoot our way through?"

"I don't have that kind of firepower," I said grimly.
Wilhelmina was almost out of bullets. I'd picked up a couple

of rifles and some ammo for them, but I preferred my own Luger for real fighting. "Besides, it's us against at least ten of them."

The police swarmed around the roadblock as if we terrified them. The battered truck hardly posed the threat of an armored personnel carrier and the sight of us inside the cab should have made them laugh, not duck for cover. Something was up. This wasn't just a random check on travel papers.

"Out! Get out with your hands up," came the command issued over a bullhorn. All the policemen hunkered down behind their Jeeps, rifles trained on us.

"Do you have any idea what's going on?" I asked Alleen.

She shrugged and said, "I'm from the Netherlands. This is all new to me. Ask me about dikes or chocolates."

"We'd better do as they say." I figured as long as they hadn't opened fire first, they might be amenable to a little jawboning. I'd swung open the protesting truck door when a single shot rang out. Ducking, I thought one of the police had gotten uptight and put a round through the truck as a warning.

Then I saw the policeman stiffen and fall forward over the barricade in the road. Seldom have I seen a man deader.

Confusion rippled through the ranks. They turned and peered into the brush on either side of the road. Then all hell broke loose. A fusilade of rifle and light machine-gun fire raked the police position. Whoever fired on the cops, had the position and the firepower to make it stick.

"Stay down. And keep the engine running," I told Alleen. Dodging, moving swiftly, I got out of the truck and ran to the barricade. Only three of the original ten police still fought. All were wounded. In the distance I heard sirens. Someone had radioed for backup. That the reinforcements were so close told me this wasn't a simple roadblock. I scooped up a fallen rifle and worked my way back to the truck.

"What're we going to do, Nick?" asked Alleen. Her voice came in a dull monotone as if the shocks she'd received in the past few days had worn her out emotionally.

"You're going to drive around the barricade and down the

road like the devil was after you." And she did.

She almost threw me out of the cab with her sudden swings around the barricade in the road. I didn't complain. I had my hands full firing the rifle. I saw nothing in the brush so I simply sprayed bullets at random. I thought I heard a cry of anguish but it might have been the squeal of tires. Whatever it was, it had to be pure luck. The guerrillas attacking the police had never shown themselves.

"Nick!"

I twisted and sat down in the cab, looking forward to see what the problem was. Men with machine guns blocked the road. I had no doubt at all that they'd use them on us if we didn't obey. It had to be part of the band ambushing the police.

"Keep driving. Run them down."

I leaned out the window and exhausted the clip in the rifle. When it became apparent we weren't going to stop, one of the guerrillas leaped up onto the running board. I used the empty rifle to smash him in the gut. He went tumbling off.

That was the signal for the others to open fire. The windshield exploded in a hail of glass splinters. Alleen squealed and tried to dodge all of them. I leaned over and kept the truck steady on the road. It was a losing battle. The bullets riddled the front end of the truck and eventually one found a tire. The explosion from behind as the tire went sent us into a long, dangerous skid that threatened to overturn us. I let Alleen handle the truck and bailed out.

She cried for me not to leave her. I had work to do.

The truck ended up against a giant Assegai tree. I hid in the low undergrowth and waited for the guerrillas to come exploring.

One passed less than two feet from me. Hugo slit his throat. I now had a bit more firepower. I took the dead guerrilla's Uzi and two spare clips. Another came. I waited. Another and another. They were dressed in camouflage suits and blended in well with their surroundings. However, no matter how well they melted into the forest, they moved clumsily. I had the impression they were a rookie unit out on their first field maneuver. They made a lot of noise crunching through the trees and several cocked and recocked their weapons nervously wasting precious ammo and making a racket a deaf man could hear.

"Out!" commanded one of the men as he took a position near the truck. "Out or we shoot!"

Alleen tumbled from the truck, battered and sporting a new set of bruises. Her once creamy flesh looked like a splotchy, pulpy brown fruit rind. But she still lived and, with any luck at all, she'd continue to do so.

"I give up," she said in that tired, beaten voice.

The guerrillas were trainees. All but one came in to peer at their captive. The one standing farthest from the group shook his head, as if in disgust at such amateurish behavior. I took him out first. The carrying strap for the Uzi dropped around his neck. A quick twist tightened the web strap and a knee in the middle of his back kept him where I wanted him. He died silently.

That left eight amateurs who'd run like hell when things went wrong.

They were harrassing Alleen, making the usual threats of raping or killing her unless she gave the information they wanted. Her listlessness puzzled them. She spoke in a flat voice and told them anything they wanted to know. They hadn't the experience yet to know if she told the truth or lied to get rid of them.

"You lie," proclaimed one, obviously destined to be a leader from his boldness in taking the initiative. When nothing came from the man I'd already killed on the perimeter, this one decided to take over entirely. He handed his machine gun to a flunky and dropped his pants. Such interrogation of female prisoners obviously aroused him. Alleen looked down at the erection and went a little whiter. "You will get what you deserve," he announced proudly.

He took one step toward Alleen. I squeezed off a single round from my captured Uzi. He got what he deserved. He clutched at his destroyed groin and rolled over and over on the ground.

For long seconds, the others didn't know what to do. They exchanged glances. I switched the Uzi to full automatic and sprayed twenty rounds in their direction. They lit out like frightened rabbits, those that still lived.

I rushed to Alleen, who had taken cover under the truck.

"Are you okay?" I asked.

"Could be better. Th-that was a good shot." Her eyes went to the man moaning, softly now, and holding where his balls had been.

"He had it coming."

"What now?"

"I follow them. We need transportation. I'm counting on them having a Jeep or truck we can use. Here, keep this. It doesn't have any recoil. Just point it like you'd point your finger and pull the trigger. I'll be back as soon as I can."

I picked up another Uzi from one of the three dead men near the truck and started through the forest at an easy lope. The guerrillas ran too fast to keep up their pace for long. I overtook them less than a mile away. They crouched together, mumbling to one another about their misfortune, which slowly turned into their great skill in escaping a party of police outnumbering them ten to one.

If they ever got back to their superiors, that story might sail. After all, their training chief had died with my web strap around his neck. No one else dared admit they didn't know the size of the force they faced. To do so would bring out that they'd run without even trying to fight.

I let them thrash about in the forest, hunting for their lost truck. When one of them strayed too far from the pack, I took him out. That left three.

They surprised me by actually finding their truck. Then they argued over how to start it. One of the fallen guerrillas had the keys; I guessed it to be the leader I'd already killed. Finally, one of them dove under the dashboard and ripped a few wires free. I hoped he knew what he was doing. I didn't want to have to rewire the damn thing if he'd screwed it up. But his misspent youth paid off. The truck protested, then turned over, the engine sounding as if it had seen better days.

I no longer needed these three.

"Help me!" I called out from cover. They exchanged looks, did a slow count, and finally realized that one of the surviving four hadn't survived after all.

I circled and waited for them to begin their hunt in the forest. When they'd gone far enough so that even a stray shot wouldn't bother me, I got into the truck and drove off.

That taught them still another lesson: never leave a vehicle unattended. Crime is rampant, even in the forest.

My sense of direction is just about perfect. I had a clear mental picture of how to get back to Alleen. Eventually I found where our first truck had smashed itself against the Assegai tree.

"Alleen!" I called. "Come on. I found us a brand new taxi."

No answer. I slipped from the truck cab and circled. Alleen would never learn. She'd gone to aid the man who'd been so intent on raping her. He now had her Uzi stuffed hard against her head.

I moved closer, not making a sound. The wind drifted through the forest, making more noise than I did. Alleen saw me. Her eyes widened a little but she gave no other sign.

The man grunted out, "Kill you, bitch. You made me less than a man. Never have children. No sons. Kill." He was in stark pain. I took care of that the instant he turned to find a more comfortable position before he killed the woman.

My stiletto flashed in the sunlight filtering through the trees. The guerrilla stiffened and fell to one side. The blade had entered between the second and third vertebrae at the base of his neck. He twitched like a beheaded snake, then ceased moving altogether.

I cleaned Wilhelmina, then checked Alleen. She looked as

if she was in shock. With all she had had to endure, it was no wonder.

We left. Alleen needed some serious psychiatric care and I couldn't give it to her. All I could do was nursemaid her until we got back to civilization.

And that wouldn't be until after I eliminated Doctor DNA.

CHAPTER TEN

My luck had changed for the better. Not only had I stolen a truck with a fair amount of gasoline in it, there were enough maps to chart me around the entire continent.

We pounded along making good time for over an hour. I felt confident about making the Namibia-South Africa border soon. According to the maps, we were less than twenty miles away.

From there, I'd have to play it by ear. I doubted we could sneak the truck across, which was a pity. That meant finding other transportation on the far side. We'd cross on foot, make our way the best we could to Windhoek, and then I'd finish my business with Faber. I only hoped my guesswork turned out to be right. Most of the time I have to operate on rumors, tenuous clues, a lot of supposition, even more intuition. Following my nose had led me directly to Bron Faber. As I'd surmised, he was Doctor DNA. Now all I could do was continue on course.

I had good feelings about Windhoek, though. Everything pointed in this direction. Faber was egomaniac enough to ignore the fact I'd tracked him down once. He'd believe he was safe and continue his operation as if nothing had happened. The best chance I had of finding him quickly lay in locating the shipping firm he used to get the metals he extorted out of Namibia and into Europe. In a country the size of Namibia, there couldn't be more than a handful of companies able to deal in such shipments.

I had good feelings about everything now. Until the bullet whined between Alleen and me.

"Damn!" I cried, swerving off the road. "Who is shooting at us now?"

"Guerrillas," the woman said. Her raven-dark hair flew in a halo around her face. She didn't even try to brush it back. Alleen simply sat, staring out the window into the sparse forest.

"You're probably right. And if they catch us, we're dead. There's no way to explain how we happen to be driving one of their trucks or how a couple of their Uzis just jumped into our hands."

I swung the truck in the other direction. The bullets came with unerring accuracy. This wasn't a fight we could drive through. Sooner or later a bullet would stop the truck.

It came sooner.

Steam rose from under the hood. The one working gauge on the dashboard—the temperature indicator—showed a meltdown approaching. One of the bullets had ruptured the radiator. I didn't care about the truck any longer, except in how it might save us. Shoving Alleen out the far side, I quickly followed her while the truck careened into a small stand of trees by the road.

I held her down in a low ditch beside the road. Aiming carefully, I let loose a burst from my Uzi. The bullets ripped through the gasoline tank on the truck. It exploded with an adequate amount of flame and noise. If the guerrillas hadn't been watching closely, they might be duped into thinking we'd been in the truck.

They weren't fooled for an instant.

"Come on," I said, tugging at Alleen's arm. "We've got to make tracks fast."

"It's no use, Nick. Let me stay."

"Run, dammit," I whispered harshly. "We've got to get away from here. I can see them already closing in."

These weren't untrained troops. They moved quickly, quietly, with confidence. I might escape them but I saw scant chance of both Alleen and me making it. Hiding the Uzis and the spare clips with some regret, I jerked hard at the dark-haired woman's arm again to snap her out of her fugue state. I doubted that she'd later remember anything about this sojourn across South Africa.

If there was a later for either of us.

"Down in the ditch, back the way we came. They won't think to look in that direction for us. Not for a few minutes."

We scooted along on our bellies, then took the chance of rising and running in a half-crouching position. No bullet ripped into my spine. I almost felt good about it until I heard the metallic *snick* of a rifle bolt closing and chambering a shell.

The mind is a wonderful computer. Mine calculated direction, distance, the way the guerrilla moved, everything. As I dived forward, Wilhelmina slipped into my hand. I twisted in midair, aimed and fired in a smooth motion. The 9mm slug found a target. The man rolled backwards, dead. His finger tensed on the trigger of his machine gun and sent a burst harmlessly into the air.

We escaped leaden death but that burst alerted the others.

Fight and die, or try to surrender and die, appeared to be the only options open.

I carried the fight to the guerrillas. Nick Carter wasn't going out with a bullet in his back while he ran.

"Stay here for a second. This might work out just fine," I

said. Out of the corner of my eye I'd caught sight of the band's leader. Tiny red epaulettes marked him as the man in charge. I used Alleen as bait while I took a position near the leader's probable approach path.

As he walked by where I hid in the tall, dry grass, I sprang. My slender-bladed knife crossed his throat, enough to let him know how close death was.

"Either use it or let me go," he said after a moment. "You have no qualms about killing." His accent came across as heavily British. I wondered if all the guerrillas had been educated at Cambridge. I asked.

"Hardly," he said. "Oxford."

"You and Sam Uwanabe must get along famously. Rowing on the Orange River."

"He was a member of the crew, wasn't he?" said the man, who finally laughed at the incongruity of the situation. "Do put down the knife. Or use it. Your companion will die, of course, if you prefer the latter course of action."

I stepped back. He rubbed across the line where Hugo had indented the skin. He turned and stared at me. The wide, round eyes missed nothing.

"You do not look as if you caused all the furor at the roadblock. Am I mistaken?"

"We got caught in the cross fire, nothing more. We want into Namibia, without having to fool around with a lot of silly regulations."

"Like travel permits?"

"Something like that, yes."

"I should kill you."

"I'm not sure Sam Uwanabe would like that."

"I'm not sure you know Sam. Using a name is easy. It means nothing. Even the police know the name."

I detailed how I'd met Uwanabe in the location outside Johannesburg.

"That changes nothing. Uwanabe's concerns are not mine."

"No, but our mission into Namibia might be."

"Explain." By this time the band—about forty guer-rillas—had gathered around. Alleen stood blank-faced and uncaring. These were confident, able men. Only topflight trickery would get me out of their hands and into Namibia safely.

"Doctor DNA," I said slowly.

"So?" But I saw the leader's reaction. I hit the right chord with him. Now all I had to do was push the advantage.

"This is a very good . . . friend," I said, indicating Alleen. "She and Doctor Faber are to be married."

"Faber? And who is this?"

I laughed. "Don't be coy. We both know who Doctor DNA is. Without him, you wouldn't get half the support you do inside Namibia. What's the take off the strategic metals reshipments? Ten million? Twenty? That kind of action keeps SWAPO going."

"We receive arms and explosives, not money."

I had him hooked.

"Will you take us to Bron?" asked Alleen, her voice quaking the smallest amount. I couldn't tell if it came from being captured or the possibility that we might again meet with her precious Bron Faber.

"We shall see. Into the brush. It will not do to be seen by police patrols."

I smiled as they herded us off. We might not be in Namibia, but it was almost as good. We were still alive and had the chance to argue some more.

"Take cover! Plane!"

We scattered and hit the dirt. The land around here looked a lot like that in the Kruger Game Preserve. The dry grassland extended flat and dusty in all directions. An aerial recon plane should be able to spot us in a second. But the guerrillas carried tarps. We ducked under them. Peering out from under the edge, I barely discerned the outlines of men huddling under another tarpaulin not ten feet away. The plane roared on its way without spotting us.

"We had not planned on returning to Namibia so soon," said Michael Zahid, the Oxford-educated guerrilla leader. "Still, aiding friends of Doctor Faber's cannot be wrong." No emotion crossed his broad face as he stared at me, and I had to wonder if he was testing me again.

"SWAPO won't be out anything by helping us," I told him.

"But will we gain?"

I shrugged.

"The border is less than a mile from here. Once you are across and into Namibia, you must find your own way. We return to patrol deep into the Union."

"I understand. And your aid is appreciated. I won't forget it."

"No," he said slowly, a smile finally crossing his lips. "I don't think *you* will forget this favor."

We hiked hard for twenty minutes over the uneven landscape and finally reached a ravine that had cut naturally under a tall fence. Alleen walked on the bottom of the ravine, her black hair never once touching the bottom strand of wire on the fence. I had to duck slightly. Otherwise, this was all it took getting into Namibia.

"Tell the good doctor that we can use more of the Uzis. The last shipment contained only two dozen. We can use twice that."

"All right, Michael. And be careful."

"I'd rather be lucky."

With that, the guerrilla leader waved his men to return into the bowels of South Africa. I wondered how much he guessed, how deep the countercurrents ran. If my hunch about SWAPO's relationship with Doctor DNA was correct, they might not want his aid much longer. Faber's power-madness shone out brightly in his every move now. He might pose grave problems for SWAPO; its leaders might decide he had become a liability to their cause.

If so, eliminating him from the game ranked high on the

things-to-do list. Michael Zahid was no one's fool. He read me perfectly. He knew my trade. If an American agent killed Faber, no repercussions could come back to haunt SWAPO from Faber's contacts. Things had worked out great for them. Not only was a threat to their power gone, it provided an opportunity to point out America's most recent covert activity, should the need arise.

Propaganda, double-dealing, duplicity, all those are part and parcel of my trade, too.

Let SWAPO take whatever propaganda coup they wanted. Removing Faber took precedence.

"Do we have to walk, Nick? My feet hurt. We've been on the go since sunrise."

"We have to hoof it until we find a likely source of transport. And out here, I doubt that will be soon."

I hate it when I'm right. We walked almost a day before a native picked us up. But the bad luck of taking so long to find mechanized transportation was offset by the man's destination. He headed for Windhoek.

Exactly where I wanted to go.

Windhoek proved a city of tedious neatness. The streets were clean enough to eat off and not a single cigarette butt or candy wrapper marred the European perfection of this windup toy of a city. We alighted on the main street and dodged the traffic. Kaiserstrasse throbbed with the lifeblood of the city: commerce. Everywhere I looked was a small shop, a pushcart selling food of all varieties, and larger stores more like those I was accustomed to seeing in Europe. The flavor of the city reminded me a great deal of Johannesburg. For all the poverty underneath, the veneer came off as stupendously wealthy.

And it should. This was one of the richest nations on earth. Copper, uranium, and diamonds provided a positive balance of trade little disrupted by the vagaries of the world economic condition. When the U.S. and other countries boomed, the copper and uranium sold well. When those metals didn't sell due to a downturn, people began panicking and the diamonds became the hedge against disaster.

Either way, Namibia prospered. And Windhoek was the hub of that prosperity.

"Where do we go, Nick?" asked Alleen.

"That's a tough question. First we find a hotel and check in. I need a shower and some food."

"I have no money."

"I've got some," I said. What I didn't tell her was my need to get in touch with Hawk. The papers in my pocket outlined how Bron Faber performed his miracles of genetic engineering on the diseases. That information had to be delivered as soon as possible. I had no contacts in Namibia and my communication gear remained behind in South Africa, but AXE has other avenues of getting vital data delivered.

"Look, Nick, look at the diamonds." She'd stopped and stared into a thick-glassed window at an array of diamond rings. "Such nice *mooi klip*," she sighed.

"What's that?"

"Pretty pebble. The first native finding a diamond, an enormous diamond, called it a pretty pebble. Bron told me my wedding ring would be the size of the Koh-i-Noor diamond. It wouldn't have been, of course, but any size would have suited me."

From the way she slowed to look in every window, I knew getting the hotel room first would be a mistake. The papers had to be passed along. And while I had some money, a sheaf more than eased the burden of checking into a hotel without luggage. I took Alleen's arm and guided her down Kaiserstrasse and away from the De Beers Diamond headquarters. At a cross street—Goeringstrasse, named after morphine addict and World War I flying ace, Hermann—we started off at right angles to the main street.

"Composers," Alleen said in a dreamy voice. "All the

streets parallel to Kaiserstrasse are named after German composers."

At Brahmstrasse, I turned again and went to the contact point. It was a CIA drop, but in this instance I was sure they wouldn't mind. Some glory reflected off them if I ran a successful mission. Next to a church noted for its neocolonial and reactionary stand, even to the point of declaring the DTA revisionist, I found the small white clapboard store I sought.

A few trinkets were scattered about the store. A tiny case of diamonds glinted in the sunlight in front. As we entered, a bell tinkled and a wizened old man emerged from behind a faded purple curtain in the back of the store.

"May I help you?" Alleen started. The man had spoken in German.

"Thanks, you can," I replied, also in German. "I would like to see what you have in the way of Bavarian cuckoo clocks."

He hesitated, eyeing me.

"Black Forest or Alpine?"

"Neither. I'd prefer to see one designed by an artist from Stuttgart."

"I have nothing like that on display. However, if you will come into the back room, there are several you might appreciate." He looked past me to Alleen, who still studied the diamonds, as if her life depended on it. This fixation kept her busy, although it hinted that her head was even more scrambled than I'd thought.

"She'll be all right alone," I said. "If we're not too long."

He held back the faded curtain for me. I almost sneezed from the dust as he opened a door little used in recent months. We sat in a room hardly larger than a closet.

"You're not CIA," he said. "You used a variation on the recognition signal."

"AXE," I said, confirming his suspicion. "I need these transmitted to David Hawk as quickly as possible." I shoved Faber's papers across the table to the nameless German shopkeeper. The papers vanished into his voluminous, over-sized jacket, as if by magic. "And I need some 9mm ammunition for my Luger." The faint smile on his lips told me this wouldn't be any problem. "And some money."

"How much? Our budget has been cut back."

"They tell me the same thing. Call it five hundred dollars, American."

"I can let you have it in D-marks. I have some South African rands, but with their inflation the way it is, European currency is better."

"Fine."

He shuffled off and returned less than a minute later with both ammunition for Wilhelmina and the money. I shoved the bullets and money into my pocket.

"I need a codename," he said.

"N3."

His posture straightened slightly. He nodded, made a notation in a small book, and motioned for me to leave. I did. There wasn't anything else to say. He knew whom he dealt with now. He didn't offend me by offering assistance. We both knew whatever he could deliver would be insignificant compared to my own abilities alone.

Sometimes the CIA and AXE can get along.

I retrieved Alleen and we went to find a hotel.

I had the uneasy feeling someone was following me. For a moment I considered a CIA tail, then decided against the idea. The old man in the store might have several operatives within Namibia, but this wasn't a large enough station to spare men to follow even a top AXE agent. What struck me as being even worse, I *thought* someone was following us but I never caught them at it.

Either my paranoia ran wild or whoever trailed me was damn good. I didn't like either alternative.

I'd left Alleen sleeping, heavily sedated, in a small hotel off Kaiserstrasse. The room was small, neat, and the clerk hadn't asked questions when we checked in. This might be a country under the control of South Africa, but the reins rested a little looser here. The clerk hadn't even asked to see our passports, something that occurs all the time even in Europe.

I carefully checked my list copied from the telephone directory. Three companies appeared to be hot prospects for shipping the metals extorted by Faber in South Africa to European ports. Two hadn't panned out. The third looked more to my liking.

A frontal assault on the secretary had gotten me little information other than the layout of the offices. Afro-European Lines, Limited, closed shop around four-thirty local time. I waited until the hard workers and brownnosers left after five. Then I went to work.

A rear window admitted me. A quick jimmy got me through to the hall. Hardly any effort at all allowed me to enter the main office. Then things got rough. The massive safe couldn't easily be opened with anything less than ten pounds of plastic explosive. I left it for last. What I needed were hints connecting the company to Faber.

I found plenty of hints in office memos and letters to the home office. I knew now that some shipping company fronted for Faber. The others I'd checked on hadn't seemed right. Afro-European did. And from the travel vouchers in front of me, that feeling had a lot of basis in reality. One of the company executives made regular trips to Walvis Bay. In and of itself, this meant nothing. Walvis Bay is the main port for Namibia.

The good part came in rental for a four-wheel vehicle while in Walvis Bay. He went to the port city three times a month—every ten days. Doctor DNA's shipments from South Africa came at that same interval. The distance between Windhoek and Walvis Bay was something less than two hundred miles. At a guess, my traveling executive worked his way about twenty miles from Walvis Bay in his four-wheeler. That covered a lot of territory, but it reduced the area considerably. I had a good shot at finding where Faber's metals shipments entered Namibia. From here, I'd have to track down the payment to him and then—bang. He'd die.

I sat in the office manager's chair as I worked through other papers, unraveling Afro-European's part in all this. While many of the details weren't available, I decided I had a clear enough picture for Hawk to put our European agents onto them.

Afro-European shipped strategic metals of all kinds. Enough hinted that they smuggled in vast quantities of illicit arms and supplies to interest all the governments involved. The stopovers at Antwerp gave it away. Belgium is one of the larger small arms producers in the world. No one had ever questioned Afro-European's shipping routes before.

Everything began to fall into place nicely. I knew who handled the metals. I knew what the payoffs were. The distance of the loading and unloading was within twenty miles of Walvis Bay. And I doubted if Faber was far away.

As I leaned back in the swivel chair, I heard a floorboard in the outer office creak. In one smooth motion, I dropped to the floor and pulled Wilhelmina from her holster. A meaty thunk echoed through the quiet room. A knife handle protruded from the middle of the leather chairback. I would've been skewered if I'd moved a fraction of a second later.

I slithered around the desk. All I saw was a shadow receding. Moving cautiously, I made it to the outer office. The door to the hallway hadn't opened. The would-be assassin remained in the room with me.

A small noise came from behind me.

I didn't turn. If I had been fooled by the ruse, I'd be dead. But the other man had committed himself. He rose and trained a gun on me. I fired first. The report almost deafened me. The man slumped forward onto the secretary's desk.

"Let's see who you are," I said, turning him over. My marksmanship is sometimes too good. I'd killed him cleanly. More information can be gained from living, breathing, talking men. Searching his pockets told me nothing. He had a 7.65mm Tokarov. I frowned. A Russian-made pistol? The man looked vaguely Balkan to me, but this meant nothing. In this country where virtually everyone came and went on foreign passports, he might be from anywhere.

"You sure do make things rough for me," I said. Grunting, I heaved the limp form over my shoulders and took him out of the office. It wouldn't do having a corpse found the next morning. I wanted them to proceed with business as usual.

Of course, the office manager might wonder how the two-inch cut in his chairback got there. But this was the only evidence I left behind.

CHAPTER ELEVEN

Getting rid of the body proved more hazardous than I'd thought. The city didn't have the roving police patrols I'd noticed in Cape Town and Johannesburg, but regular policing began on the streets after sunset. Explaining how I just happened to have a dead Balkan citizen slung over my shoulder might be on the difficult side.

What made matters even worse, the feeling of being watched, of being tailed, still persisted. I'd thought the dead man had been the one so hot to follow. Now I couldn't be sure.

I dropped him in an alley behind the offices of Afro-European Lines and stepped into the street. Glancing up and down told me there wasn't any way I'd get the body out unless I wanted to create an international incident. Leaving him in the alley might be equally as dangerous, too. The police checked regularly, probably looking for SWAPO terrorists or drunks.

Tapping out a cigarette, I turned and pretended to study the contents of a nearby shop window as I lit it. A man walked by, not giving me a second glance. However, his face rang all sorts of bells in my mind. His last name was Korchov. The first name eluded me at the moment, but he definitely belonged in the Third Directorate of the KGB—one of their agents assigned to England.

Or had been. Now he walked the streets of Windhoek.

The dead Balkan, Korchov—what was going on? It looked like a spy convention in Namibia.

"Don' worry, he didn' see you," came the quiet words from behind. I jumped in surprise. I hadn't been paying attention, and the man had simply walked up on me.

"Achmed!" I cried. "You know him?"

"Bela Korchov? Yes, of course I do. Recently transferred here from London. He feels it is a demotion. I've approached him."

"For what organization?" I asked suspiciously.

"Why MI-5, of course. We Britishers haven't totally dug a hole and pulled it in after us when the sun set on our Empire."

British intelligence. Achmed ben-Gorra. Other pieces to the puzzle fell into place.

"You're lucky to be alive," I said.

"I know. Many thanks for that boffo performance aboard *The Easy Ride*. I'm not sure I could have captured the tsetse fly as easily as you, old chap."

The Bantu aboard the ship had been sent to kill an undercover agent, all right. Only he'd been sent to eliminate Achmed, not me. My cover had been intact then. Achmed's had been blown. That explained why Faber didn't recognize me when we met in Johannesburg. He thought the foreign agent after him had been eliminated—and I hardly fit Achmed's description. Faber had suspected me, but not as being the agent aboard *The Easy Ride*.

"Seems one of our chaps got careless in contacting me. Faber's men are damn fine. A shame wasting them on him."

"You don't even sound like a sailor now," I marveled.

"Hard work. I think I'll put in for a bit of desk work after this is over." He cocked his head and studied me. "You need help getting rid of surplus baggage?"

I nodded in the direction of the alley.

Achmed motioned. A large black cab swung up to the curb. He opened the back door and said, "Do help your friend in."

I struggled with the now stiff body. Rigor mortis makes it almost impossible to handle a body easily. I finally dumped the corpse in the back. Achmed restrained me from getting in. He slammed the door and the cab roared off into the twilight.

"Let me handle this. This makes us even. You saved my life aboard ship, whether you knew it or not, and now I am performing a favor for you."

"Done." I shook hands on it.

"This is getting to be a quite crowded place," he said, as we walked slowly in the direction opposite to that taken by Korchov. "I've spotted a veritable stew of agents boiling about. Seems Faber has stirred up an anthill with his extortion scheme."

"And?" I pressed.

"And?" Achmed said, one eyebrow arching slightly. "You haven't heard, then? I doubt there's a government leader in the world he hasn't threatened with rather horrible death if they don't obey his every command. He has carried through with a few minor officials, much to their displeasure, I might say."

Faber had finally gone off the deep end. As long as he restricted his activities to South Africa, not many of the world leaders would have cared much, at least in private. If anything, it might have meant better bargaining levers with the country. Now that he'd carried his mad dreams of world conquest into the international arena, he became a prize target for any and all.

"At least five different countries have agents wandering around Windhoek looking for him."

"Why here?" I asked.

"You're here," pointed out Achmed. "The shipping company has hardly maintained a low profile. You discovered it in less than a day's effort. Don't discount the rest of us."

I debated the merit of working with Achmed on this. His contacts might prove beneficial, but something held me back. The British were as staunch an ally as we had in the world. But that didn't mean their best interests coincided with those of the United States.

"Then again," Achmed went on, "my superiors back in London might not let me stick around here much longer. Seems they want to pull in the horns. Protect all the good folks."

"They've been doing that quite a while against the IRA." But I saw what Achmed was doing. He gave me an out if I wanted to pursue Doctor DNA on my own.

I did.

In this business you should never get personal. Grudges lead to mistakes. Revenge is something without sanction by the higher-ups. And I still wanted Bron Faber for my own. Something about him got to me. What he'd done to Alleen was only part of it. The woman wouldn't be the same again, not without a considerable amount of time with a shrink. At this point, I'd be better off professionally letting Achmed carry on. I was the one who should be thinking about cashing in and going home, not the tall British agent.

"I'll work alone on this," I heard myself saying. In spite of all the rational, logical, *good* reasons against it, I heard myself telling him I'd forge on ahead.

"Do keep in touch, old boy. If you need any backup, let me know."

"Thanks. One last thing, Achmed."

"Yes?"

"How many other KGB agents are in Windhoek right now? Korchov is topnotch. Have the Soviets run in another?"

"You mean the one you snuffed in the Afro-European

offices? No, he was an independent. I believe he represented Turkey or Cyprus, one of those middlin' small powers in that area.''

''Turkey?''

''Faber left out no one when he issued his demand to be the new king of the world.''

''I see. I'd best get back to see how Alleen is doing.''

''Faber's intended?''

I ignored the question. He knew damn well who she was.

''Be seeing you, Achmed. And thanks again.''

''Cheerio!''

I made a few moves designed to throw off anyone following me, more out of habit than conviction. If Achmed had been the one trailing me before, he already knew what hotel I stayed in. The man might know even more than that, in fact. I figured he wanted to go it alone. Agents have egos, too. From what I'd seen of Achmed, he was a big man and probably had needs to match.

I looked in on Alleen. She still slept her drugged sleep. I silently closed the door and sat in the best chair in the sitting room. The suite had cost much less than I'd thought and the service here matched what I'd found in South Africa. So much for the good news. I leaned my head back and rested it on the top edge.

Before I realized it, I was asleep.

A sharp knock on the door jarred me awake.

I called out, ''Who's there?''

''Mail, sir,'' came the reply.

I checked Hugo's position on my right forearm, sure that he wouldn't fail me. Then I opened the door. It's better to be safe than sorry. In this case, my preparations amounted to overly cautious behavior. The small, fair, sandy-haired bell-hop had a small package sent to me from my ''uncle'' in South Africa. I thanked the man and gave him a couple of D-marks. He smiled and left.

Ripping off the paper revealed what I'd hoped to find.

Hawk had sent a television communicator device. After checking to see that Alleen still slept, I attached the device, knowing I could talk undisturbed for some time yet. The set warmed up, the picture scrambled, and then flowed into familiar outlines.

Hawk sat with his perennial cigar firmly locked in the corner of his mouth. His jaw set at an angle that told me this call hadn't gone through an instant too soon. If I hadn't called, I might have found the man personally banging on my door. Over the years I've learned to spot the ominous signs. This one wasn't a good one, of that I was positive.

"Yes, sir?" I asked.

"It's Doctor DNA, N3," he said without preamble. "He's moved against the government leaders in four European countries. I feel this isn't a serious attempt on his part."

"What's 'not serious' mean, sir?"

"Only four ministers were killed. He could have taken out the upper echelons. Instead, he opted to remove lower-ranking bureaucrats as a show of his power. Two died from sleeping sickness, one from yellow fever, and one simply rotted away in front of a crowd of reporters. He was a press secretary."

"And Faber called all the deaths?"

"He released word to the world press. Up till now, no one had heard of him. They assumed he was just another crank and ignored him. Now he gets front page coverage every time he says 'Boo!' I want him stopped *now*, N3.

"Who has he contacted in the United States?"

"The ranking officer in each branch of our armed forces, the Speaker of the House, the Vice President, and the President himself. None is amused, N3."

I took a deep breath. Things had moved faster than I thought, but I had a few aces up my sleeve. Faber couldn't know I'd gotten on his trail again so quickly. Then again, it might not matter if he knew I was here or not. The entire city of Windhoek swarmed with agents. Agents of Korchov's caliber wouldn't take long to find the clues I already had in my possession.

"Is there any way of protecting them, sir?"

"Of course."

When Hawk didn't say any more, I knew that matters had indeed become serious. I didn't have "a need to know" so he wasn't going to even mention it. Still, I had to smile. The vision of the White House adorned with flypaper struck me as ludicrous.

"I need some support, sir. The CIA drop was fine in an emergency, but I don't wish to . . . impose."

"Certainly not. If I understand your report correctly, the best place for additional aid is not in Windhoek but in Walvis Bay. Is that correct, N3?"

"Yes, sir, it is. I want to take Alleen along, too."

"As a lightning rod? You might draw more fire than the ploy is worth, Nick."

"I realize the risk I'm taking. But she seems attuned to Faber in some way I don't understand. Her entire world has been shattered by the man, yet she keeps on with her fantasy of him marrying her."

"She is unstable. That spells even more trouble for you. Leave her in the hotel. Our men will attend to her."

"I'd prefer to keep her on, as I've outlined. I know the base Faber uses is within twenty miles or so of Walvis Bay. Alleen might be able to give me a clue as to where within that radius the laboratory is."

"By the way, N3," Hawk said in a low voice. "Our agents have examined the laboratory out on the veldt in the Kruger Game Preserve. Good work. All the flies were killed and no shred of evidence remained. Do as well with the recombinant DNA/disease lab and I'll see that you get a nice, long R & R."

"Thanks," I said dryly. Whenever Hawk dished out promises like that, it meant the job had little chance of being easy. The AXE computers had been cranking out projections; while Hawk would never reveal them to me, I guess they gave me small hope of success. Not only did I compete with agents from other countries, I might find myself up to my hip pockets in other AXE agents.

Or then again, maybe not. Hawk had confidence in me and might not want me hindered with others. I wouldn't ask what his decision was either way.

The last glimpse I had of Hawk was him tossing away his cigar stub and lighting up a fresh stogie. The blue-green clouds of noxious vapor swirled around his face just as the television screen went to all-white.

I sighed and leaned back in my chair. It was time to rouse Alleen and go to work again.

The return to Walvis Bay was as inauspicious as my first trip here. This time, instead of being a sailor, I posed as a tourist from Germany. My fluent German stood me in good stead and took away some of the anti-American sting I'd felt from my inquiries. Traveling with Alleen, who was obviously Dutch, helped immeasurably. I've long since learned the easy way to get through a customs line in any country is to be immediately in front of a beautiful woman.

The customs agents are so much in a hurry to get to the woman that they'll miss small items. In my case, those small items were my Luger and stiletto, plus a powerful little radio for communicating with AXE headquarters half the world away.

Alleen followed me through the customs line. It took me less than two minutes to clear. They held her up for over fifteen minutes. In other circumstances the ingratiating, persistent official might have wrangled the name of her hotel or some local address from her, but the dark-haired woman still just . . . drifted.

The psychiatrists call it a fugue state. She lived and breathed and acted, but only if pushed into it by someone else. By herself, Alleen was little more than a lifelike department-store dummy. Occasional flashes of animation occurred, notably when she saw something that triggered memories concerning Bron Faber.

Diamonds. That did it. White dresses. That did it, too. But otherwise she just existed, never volunteering anything and talking only when I directed a question specifically at her.

In the taxi, I sat close to her, holding her hand. It hung limp and dry as if it belonged to a lizard rather than a human being.

"We're going to find the local office for Afro-European Lines," I told her as soon as we'd gotten out of the customs shed. No response. "I'm hoping from there we can get a line on Bron."

"Bron's there?" she asked. "He never mentioned any Afro-European Company to me."

"What about his shipping? You said something once about him having a lot of shipments from Cape Town to Walvis Bay."

"Yes, he mentioned that."

"And?" I tired easily of having to force every syllable from her shell-shocked mind.

"Swakopmund," she said, as if the word tasted bitter on her lips.

I leaned back in the seat and thought. Swakopmund was a small port city just to the north of Walvis Bay. Walvis Bay was hardly the biggest deep-water port in the world. Swakopmund beat it out on the list for world's smallest. Without a lot of government inspectors, it might be perfect for Faber's metal shipments.

I sighed. The South African government had done very little right in this matter. They might have stopped Faber a lot sooner than I could have if they'd played their cards right: given in to the extortion demands, planted transmitters in the shipment, followed it, and then used their political clout to crack down on Afro-European Lines and others involved in getting the metals to a smelter in Europe. They'd panicked, tried to keep the plague a secret, had tried to be all things to all people. As a result, ministers died, Faber went on unchecked, and it took an outsider—me—to find out the details of the scheme.

The South Africans didn't even know AXE had come onto the case, either. That was for the best. I wondered if they realized the British, the Russians, and the agents of probably a half-dozen other countries were filtering into their territory to take care of Faber. I doubted it. The more a state relies on its police, the less likely it is to admit that anything can go wrong.

I had to admit to being lucky in having Alleen along with me. This eliminated a lot of the legwork that I'd planned on. The name "Swakopmund" alone told me the location of Faber's illicit trafficking. A twenty-mile radius of Walvis Bay would have taken a good length of time to explore. Now all I had to cover was a small sector.

"Here's the place you want, mister," called out the cabbie. I handed him five marks for the ride and helped Alleen out. Leaning in the window, I gave the cabbie another ten, saying, "Take our bags to the Hotel Dreifontein."

"You betcha," he said. I cringed at the Americanism, then smiled. He roared off. I had a brief pang of suspicion that the cabbie might keep both the money and our luggage, then I put it from my mind. I had all I needed to survive on. Wilhelmina rested snugly under my arm and my stiletto sheathed firmly on my right forearm.

"What are we doing here?" asked Alleen, staring at the plain stuccoed front of Afro-European Lines, Limited. She didn't seem to remember any of the trip in the taxi, and the taxi was barely out of sight down the street.

"Just getting an added line on Bron. I don't want you saying anything while I'm inside, okay?"

"Yes, Nick."

I had the feeling she would obey as long as I promised her a chance to see Faber again. I shook my head. She'd been abused in about every way possible and something still lurked inside her that cared for, even loved, Bron Faber.

He didn't deserve it.

"I'm Herr Steiner from the home office," I said, introducing myself to the receptionist. The woman's expression told me that I was not expected, which figured. I hadn't intended on trying this unless I was really sure of myself. With Alleen's lead to Swakopmund, any small confirmation would do me.

"From Dusseldorf?" the woman asked, her face turning even whiter. "But you were not expected. Were you?"

"I hope not. This is a snap inspection. The chairman of the board feels it necessary to maintain good field discipline. I will see your travel vouchers now."

"Yes, of course, right away." I wanted to laugh at the way she opened the files to me. I had about five minutes before the initial shock wore off and she found one of her bosses. That might be about all it'd take to run down the travel vouchers filed on this end by the executive from Windhoek. "And get me a cup of coffee right away."

My tone came out harsher than I expected, but brow-beating the woman got me what I wanted. Before she had returned with the coffee, I had my information.

The four-wheel vehicle rental company, the duration of rental and—jackpot!—a destination report.

Alleen had been right. Faber used Swakopmund as his trans-shipment point.

"This coffee is bitter. Is your superior in?"

"Herr Richter? He, that is . . ."

"Never mind. I shall return in one hour. Exactly one hour. At that time I desire a meeting with Richter and all of his assistants. Arrange it." With that, I took Alleen's arm, guided her out of the office and away from the Afro-European offices.

"What are we doing, Nick?" she asked. "Is this helping us find Bron?"

"Yes."

"Can we go to the hotel now? I . . . I'd like to freshen up."

We went back to the hotel while I arranged for a Jeep. I was on my way to tracking down Doctor DNA and permanently removing him and the threat he posed to the world. I didn't burden Alleen with that knowledge, though. I let her shower, dress for bush country, and think her reunion with her be-trothed would be all sweetness and light.

It amazed me how well she forgot everything bad that had happened to her. I hadn't. And that's what counted.

The cargo ship creaked under the strains put on its hull by the immense load of ore it carried. I pushed Alleen down behind a bush not a hundred yards from the docking area. Longshoremen moved with lazy grace, both anticipating and dreading the work ahead. When the ship had finally docked and men swarmed like ants around it, I began looking elsewhere, hoping to catch sight of Faber. I didn't know if he personally supervised the shipment or whether he left it to the SWAPO guerrillas.

Apparently, he left it to the guerrillas. Men with Uzis stood around watching every approach to the dock. If any government inspector chanced on this small transaction, he'd die quickly. I had no doubt his body would be dumped at sea as the cargo ship returned to Cape Town.

"Is he here, Nick? Do you see him anywhere?"

Alleen had become fanatical about seeing Bron again. I quietly told her that only his assistants worked here tonight.

"But will we find him?"

"I think we will. See that man over there? The one smoking the cigarette?" A tiny orange coal gleamed in the blackness of shadows cast by a building. "He's the overseeer."

"How can you tell?"

"I just can." I didn't want to get into a long, involved description of how he held his body, how he talked to the others, and how they talked to him. He was the leader.

It took almost two hours to unload the ore. I couldn't tell from here what type of strategic metal ore it was, and it didn't matter. I needed to see the next portion of the transaction. Over an hour elapsed before the cargo ship left this makeshift port and another, even larger ship docked. This time the unloading consisted of small crates.

Small arms. Ammunition. Explosives. The way the man I pegged as leader came forward told me all I needed to know about the contents of the boxes. He quickly dispatched his men to loading them onto battered trucks similar to the ones I'd already seen used by SWAPO out in the forests and on the veldt. Then he talked with the cargomaster. Money changed hands. And I was almost taken by surprise when the guerrilla spun and suddenly left.

He'd been paid off. He'd gotten his pound of flesh. Loading the ore onto this ship was something the sailors had to do. The SWAPO guerrillas were done for the evening, weapons and money in hand.

"Stay here," I said to Alleen. As silently as a shadow, I pursued the guerrilla leader. He stood with several of his men next to a truck, chatting, smoking cigarettes, and divvying up the money.

Four of them. And the one I needed most—the leader—wasn't likely to go off by himself so I could get at him. I felt the pressure of time and decided to make the move now. In any mission one key action puts everything into motion, for better or for worse. This was it.

I walked boldly up to the guerrillas. Rifles came up. I heard the bolt of the leader's Uzi snapping shut. I kept walking until I was less than five feet from the tiny group.

"Pardon me, chaps, I'm looking for someone to put me in touch with Doctor DNA." The fraction of a second that went by as surprise took hold gave me the time I needed for action. My foot found a groin. Hugo slipped between another's ribs. I batted away a rifle barrel aimed for my head, and drove my fist into an exposed throat. And then I faced the leader.

His machine gun came up. Everything moved in slow motion then. If only the rest of the world had turned into molasses, I'd've been fine. But no matter how hard I pushed, my own limbs felt as if I forced them through water. The adrenaline rush speeded up my perceptions but did nothing to aid my reflexes.

I watched as his lips pulled back in a grimace. His knuckle turned white as it tightened on the trigger. But I noticed his stance wasn't square, braced, ready for swift movement.

I lunged to one side. Again, I felt as if impossible weights held me back. But the slugs ripped air just inches over my head. And I'd dodged in the right direction. The Uzi has little recoil, but it's an automatic weapon with all the faults physics gives to automatics. The muzzle lifted up and to the right as I faced it—I'd gone left.

Getting inside the guerrilla leader's guard was easy then. Off balance, he couldn't move. My knife slashed across his wrists. The machine gun fell from lifeless, useless hands. Hugo's sharp blade had severed arteries and tendons.

"Aieee!" he shrieked. "Allah be merciful! My hands!"

"Your throat will go next if you make even one small noise." I pressed the sharp tip of the stiletto into his Adam's apple. A tiny strangled noise emerged from his lips. That was all. "Good," I said. "Let's get out of here. If you want to keep on living, don't make a sound."

He obeyed well. He clutched his severed wrists the best he could, then realizing neither hand staunched the flow of the other, thrust them under his arms and squeezed down. Blood leaked out and down the sides of his body, soaking his dirty khaki shirt.

"I am dying," he protested. "I will bleed to death."

"Just stay like that. It takes a while to bleed to death from cut wrists. First you get cold, then sleepy. You still look feverish to me. You've got a ways to go. Maybe you'll even survive the night—if you cooperate."

He sat in a huddled lump in the alley I'd chosen. Piles of garbage and excrement belied knowledge of any modern sanitation system. The Germanic efficiency shown in Windhoek and even Walvis Bay didn't extend this far out into the boondocks, it seemed. But this made a perfect spot to interrogate my captive.

"You're SWAPO," I said.

"You are not with the police?"

"I couldn't care less about Namibia's internal policies. Or South Africa's. I want information about your boss, Doctor DNA."

"He is not my boss. I am a freedom fighter." For a moment, the recited propaganda gave him the adrenaline rush needed to wave his hands about. The shower of blood convinced him against any more outbursts.

"I don't care what you call him or what you think you're doing. In exchange for unloading his ore shipments and seeing that they're on an Afro-European Lines ship bound for

Europe, you get paid off in arms and money. I want to talk with him."

No answer.

"Getting cold yet? Your color's not too good." The guerrilla had turned a pasty gray color under his natural chocolate skin. The effect was not pleasant.

"I know nothing of this Doctor DNA."

"I can afford to wait on this one," I said, leaning casually against a dirty, graffiti-written wall. "You can't."

He glared at me. The anger drove out his fear, but only for a few seconds. Then he worked his wrists up and down against his body. A fresh stream of blood leaked out to dampen his chest.

"You will kill me anyway. No matter what I say, you will kill me."

"That might be the way the Democratic Turnhalle Alliance police learned from their South African friends, but it's not the way I operate. If you give me the information I want, I'll see that an ambulance is sent for you."

"They'd kill me."

"You're going to die here and now. Maybe you can get away from them. I don't know. Want to match one hundred percent chance of dying with me against some unknown percent with the authorities?"

"What do you want to know?" I swear his teeth rattled. I didn't think it was fear; it had to be the coldness of bleeding to death setting in.

"Where's Doctor DNA's headquarters? They're somewhere nearby. I need to know exactly where."

"The doctors? You won't forget?"

"Forget? Tell me and I'll contact the hospital immediately."

"I'm cold," he said, shaking. "And so tired."

"Doctor DNA," I prodded. "Where?"

"In the jungle. Outside of town. Ten miles, no more. Go east. Marked road to Windhoek. Ten miles, no more. No more . . ." He slumped over, unconscious.

I considered what he'd said. It fit the pattern I'd noticed

with Faber. On the road to Windhoek provided ground transport. So near Swakopmund gave him access to the shipping lanes. Yeah, it all fit.

Dropping beside the man, I tore off bloody strips from his shirt and bound his cut wrists to close the wounds. On my way back to where I'd left Alleen, I found a pay telephone and called the nearest hospital, giving them directions and what had happened. Whether or not they responded, I don't know. I didn't stay around to find out.

Doctor Bron Faber and his disease lab were only ten miles away. I wanted to finish this mission as quickly and efficiently as possible.

CHAPTER TWELVE

I parked the Jeep about five hundred yards down the road from the small white sign I'd seen declaring, "Medical Research Center." Faber's egomania roared out again. No one intent on conquering the world would advertise his presence with a sign unless totally separated from his senses. In a way, he was as out of touch with reality as Alleen. They made a pretty pair.

I glanced at the woman. She sat quietly, hands folded in her lap. She hadn't seen the sign. She hardly noticed I'd stopped the Jeep and gotten out. I·debated about my best course of action. Leaving her was the only logical thing to do. I couldn't have her looking over my shoulder, yet it hardly seemed proper to let her sit alone like that in the Jeep. If anything out of the ordinary happened, she might go flying off into a panic from which she might not return.

Still, I had my job to think about. It came first. Killing Bron Faber was top priority.

"I won't be long, Alleen," I said, resting my hand on her arm. She turned to face me, a tiny smile lurking on her lips.

"What? Oh, yes, of course, Nick. You won't be long."

"You'll stay here, won't you?"

"Yes, Nick."

This time I was sure I'd made a mistake about the raven-tressed beauty. She was better off in Windhoek or Walvis Bay, yet I couldn't take the time to send her back. And allowing her to travel alone had too many problems attached to it. Not only wasn't she in any shape to be left alone, the foreign agents rattling around Namibia would pick up on her in an instant. They weren't stupid; they'd have good descriptions of her as being connected with Faber. Some, like Achmed, would seize on the opportunity to upstage me. No. Alleen would stay where she was.

I cast one last look back at her before entering the woods. The ironwood trees sparsely covered the land. The sneeze-wood trees were more prevalent and caused me no end of trouble. By the time I'd gotten to a small clearing with a single building in the center, my nose was stopped up and my eyes watered continuously. Dabbing at the allergic reactions did no good.

I blew my nose and wiped my eyes clear.

And saw victory ahead.

In the doorway of the building stood Bron Faber wearing a white lab smock that gently flapped in the soft breeze blowing through the clearing. He held one of his magic wands for controlling his tsetse flies. He didn't seem to aim it in my direction, which meant I had at least one good shot at the man.

Wilhelmina came into my hand. I quickly pulled back the toggles. The slide jacked up into the air, arching its metallic back, then slid forward in a smooth action that carried a 9mm Parabellum round into the chamber. I sighted.

And I didn't like the sight-picture.

Faber stared directly at me. And he smiled. My finger came back on the Luger's hair trigger. The shot went wide by a foot when a powerful blow landed on the back of my neck. I went down, stunned, but somehow kept the automatic in my grip. The world wildly spun around me and stars glowed in hazy, nebulous constellations. It hardly seemed possible what had happened to me.

I'd been attacked by a gorilla. It bounced up and down not five feet away.

Those beasts have gotten lousy press. They're vegetarians, shy, and run whenever man comes near. In fact, this shyness has led to their virtual extinction throughout Africa. Very seldom do they use those prodigious muscles to fight. They run—and are run off their territorial breeding grounds.

"Wha—?" was all I managed to say before the gorilla lumbered forward, long, incredibly powerful arms outstretched. I hardly believed this was happening to me. This normally shy animal wanted my scalp.

I fired point-blank. Again. And again. Then a mighty hand batted Wilhelmina from my grip.

I heard Faber's distant laughter. Turning to look at him, slow understanding dawned. He held his guidance wand and pointed it in my direction. He controlled the gorilla with it. The man had experimented on more than simple insects. He'd managed to genetically alter a mountain gorilla and turn it into a killer.

Even worse, it killed at his command.

"Die, Carter," came the mocking words. "My little pet will even ease you into a shallow grave. He's quite handy around here—for getting rid of the garbage!"

Three 9mm slugs hadn't even inconvenienced the animal. Tiny spots on its chest oozed blood where the bullets had entered, but not so anyone would notice. The impact of the slugs went unnoticed, too, because of the creature's bulk. It could take incredible shocks and keep on going. I prayed that one of the bullets had found its way into a vital organ, a liver, a kidney, across an artery. I hoped for internal damage. The beast certainly didn't pay any attention to its wounds as it swung toward me, its tiny red eyes radiating a hatred that bordered on the human.

"Nice, gorilla," I said, inching away. I got to my feet.

Tensing my right arm I sent Hugo racing down into my hand. I stabbed out just as the giant gorilla lunged. The sharp blade slashed through a furry arm. The gorilla recoiled and bellowed in pain. I wasn't so sure I'd done the right thing after all. I'd only enraged him.

It lunged again.

Humans have survived in the worst of conditions against stronger predators through agility and intelligence. I used agility now. Ducking those powerful, crushing arms, I darted out and into the forest. There was no way in hell I could outmuscle that beast.

"Don't quit on me now, feet," I muttered, as my legs pumped to put distance between the gorilla and myself.

When I'd put enough distance between us, I stopped and panted like a dog in the sun. I hadn't counted on the gorilla's strong arms and being in terrain custom-made for it. The simian had swung through the trees using long, powerful arms. The creature was so well-adapted to this kind of country it had easily outmatched my fleet pace on the ground.

I again faced the beast.

"Easy, now," I said, beginning to circle. I held my knife in front of me, knowing this was little more than a crutch for me now. Still, it was my best weapon. I tried to talk to the beast in a low, soothing voice, hoping to lull him a bit.

Whatever Faber's magic wand did to the animal, it did too damned well. The gorilla attacked.

I kept Hugo between us—then the blade went into the beast's chest. Arms twice as long as mine circled my body and held me firmly to that hard, hairy chest. The grip on my knife slipped; the blade remained inside the animal as he began applying more and more power to the back-breaking grip he held me in.

I felt the breath gusting from my lungs. The gorilla fought like a boa constrictor. As soon as I exhaled, it tightened up a little more on its crushing embrace. I slowly suffocated because my chest muscles weren't strong enough to allow me to draw a good lungful of air against the inexorable tightening. Struggling, wiggling, kicking, I fought to get one arm free.

Even as I did, I felt the world turning black. Everything spun crazily about me. My pulse pounded harshly in my temples. No oxygen made it into my lungs.

I poked my thumb directly into the gorilla's left eye. With an agonized howl, the animal dropped me. I kicked free and rolled and kept rolling. The world changed from black to red as my tortured lungs fought to suck in as much oxygen as possible. I was getting too much air. Brain came into control over body. I held my breath until I felt the red curtain I'd seen being pulled away. Then I panted again, letting the life-giving oxygen flood my lungs once more.

I hardly had time to regain my breath before the gorilla attacked again. In my weakened condition, one more lover's hug from the gorilla would kill me. My spine ached and popped in protest every time I moved. I have a strong back; but compared to the strength mustered by the gorilla, I was like a newborn baby.

I slipped backward into the woods. I wanted a sturdy tree trunk between us. Out-dodging it seemed a likely tactic to try. Nothing else I could do had a ghost of a chance of working for very long. I had nothing to lose but my life by trying it.

The resounding roar as he attacked shook me. Animals don't usually cry when on the attack. That's either before or after the hunt. Still, I had to remember that Faber had geneti-cally engineered this animal to his own specifications. He'd wanted a killer. There wasn't any need for that juggernaut to be silent.

I kicked at precisely the right instant. I caught the gorilla on a kneecap. It went down, rolled easily, and came up again, unhurt. Hugo still stuck in the animal's ribs. As soon as it charged again, I dashed around a tree, ducked down, and spun. I grabbed hold of the knife handle and twisted.

Rage.

I regained possession of my knife.

This time I played a very dangerous game. I allowed the gorilla to encircle my body with those long, deadly arms. I'd sucked in as much air as I could in hopes of hyperventilating. What I had to do might take more than a single lungful of air.

"Aieee!" I shrieked as the gorilla's arms smashed down into my body. For a moment, all thought of my battle plan slipped away in pain. Then I brought my elbows down into the gorilla's shoulders. It felt as if I smashed into stone. The muscles overlaying the beast's upper back and shoulders tensed into steely immobility.

I felt the world going away again. Not enough oxygen. I stabbed out with Hugo. The sharp blade cut down into the gorilla's shoulders. Nothing. I cut and slashed and hacked like some apprentice butcher. Blood spattered all over now but nothing lessened the bone-mangling grip around my body.

Inexorably, life fled my body. I jabbed down again, the point striking the juncture between head and torso. I couldn't find a neck. Blackness welled up and swept over me. I feebly stabbed over and over. It might as well have been a mosquito's sting against a dinosaur.

I don't remember passing out.

I barely remember coming to, the heavy weight pressing down onto my body. Breathing was almost impossible. I checked to make sure that the word "impossible" wasn't absolutely true. My mouth and nostrils were filled with a stinking fur coat. Turning my head, fresh air came in again.

It took long minutes for me to understand what had happened. Even as I blacked out, I had stabbed down with my knife. One of those thrusts had found the gorilla's carotid artery. It had bled to death in less time than it took for the gorilla to crush the life from me. Obviously. I still lived, it didn't.

As it collapsed, it carried me forward. Its weight held me down. Its dead weight.

Another minute passed before I found the strength to work

out from under that mountain of dead meat. I was covered in blood—not mine.

But I lived.

And, all things considered, I wasn't in too bad shape. My ribs hurt like hell. Maybe one or two were cracked but nothing broken, no compound fractures with naked white bone protruding through the skin. My lungs wheezed and protested a steady, regular, constant flow of air. They'd adjust back to normal soon enough. And while other muscles ached horribly, I was in one piece.

Bron Faber had just a bit more to pay for now.

I backtracked the path of my wild retreat from the gorilla. I found crushed grass and broken limbs on low-hanging trees. Then I found Wilhelmina. I checked the action to make sure no dirt had gotten into the works. Lugers are precision machines. They work reliably and well under adverse conditions, but dirt or sand in the slide will cause one to jam. The last thing in the world I wanted now was for my gun to jam at a critical moment.

I'd missed Faber once today. I wouldn't miss twice, no matter what he sent against me.

I advanced on the building, doing a sneak-up to keep from alerting him. And again it didn't work.

Faber appeared in the doorway, his wand in hand.

"Carter? You amaze me," he said in a mildly agitated tone. "You got away from the gorilla. Well, never mind. Do come inside. I think you'll find what I have to show you very instructive."

I raised my Luger for the shot that would take him out. I stopped in time to keep from missing once more. He'd vanished into the building. I followed.

In my haste to dispatch the mad scientist, I got careless. I stalked into the room, my pistol leading the way. If anything had moved, it would have gotten a couple of slugs instantly. But nothing living moved. The door slammed behind me, pulled shut with a slender wire leading outside. In a flash, I realized there wasn't a doorknob inside. The windows were screened over with heavy metal wire-mesh, and the only other door to the room was on the far side—and closing.

"Good-bye for good this time, Carter. My faithful allies will not make the same mistake the gorilla did." Faber's taunting voice came from outside. He'd tugged on the wire that closed the door, trapping me in this crackerbox of a room. Given enough time, I'd be out of here and after him.

Faber didn't give me that time.

Swarms of the tsetse flies gushed up from a box the man had opened before leaving the room. There was no way I could get through the heavy screens over the windows fast enough to keep from perishing. Doubtlessly, these flies were infested with the worst diseases Faber could concoct.

Instinct saved me. I didn't have time to logically think it through. I simply acted. Slashing through my pants leg revealed Pierre. The tiny gas bomb hung intact on my inner thigh. I sucked in a deep breath, then mashed the grenade. Odorless, invisible nerve gas billowed forth. I felt the grenade turning cold against my skin; the gas is highly compressed. As it gushed forth, it expanded and cooled to the point that tiny ice crystals formed on my flesh.

But I didn't worry about a little frostbite. I worried that the tsetse flies would not be affected by the gas quickly enough to keep them from swarming on me, biting me, killing me.

I swatted one and crushed it. Gingerly, I wiped its blood off my skin using a rag I found on a nearby wooden work table. All the while my ears filled with the buzzing of deadly insects, I felt my lungs protesting. All AXE agents can hold their breaths for four minutes—under normal conditions.

I felt as if someone had taken baseball bats to my ribcage. The gas released from Pierre dissipates in about three minutes. I'd only gone two and already felt dizzy. My lungs threatened to explode unless I took a nice, deep breath.

If I did, Pierre would kill me. My own faithful companion would slay me even faster than a bullet through the brain.

The buzzing sounded louder, more insistent. The nerve gas didn't work against tsetse flies. I fought to reach a window, to begin ripping out the heavy mesh screening. Sinking to my knees, I knew I couldn't go on any longer. Not even three minutes had elapsed and the buzzing sounded like the roar of a huge crowd.

"Nooo!" I gasped. And nothing happened. I pressed my nose close to the screen and inhaled. Fresh air. All of Pierre's nerve gas had dissipated. The cross-ventilation had cleared it out sooner than I'd thought.

As I sucked in life-giving air, I noticed the buzzing went away. The gas *had* killed the tsetse flies; all I'd heard buzzing was the blood roaring in my own head.

I didn't move for several minutes. I wanted to be sure I was back into fighting trim—or something close to it. I'd run across two of Faber's genetically mutated inventions today and had bested both. But the cost to me physically was great. Settling my mind helped. I pictured myself sinking into a pool of warm, clear water. The ripples expanded outward and soothed, calmed, renewed. By the time I pulled myself erect and faced the middle of the room, I felt like I could take on both a gorilla and a swarm of tsetse flies at the same time.

"You bastard," I muttered softly. I walked to the door and studied it. The doorknob had been removed and a plate welded over the receptacle. I checked out the other door. Same thing. Carefully studying the entire door frame, I decided against forcing my way out this route. The best way appeared to be cutting into the screen and pulling it back far enough to snake through.

My knife nicked and dulled as I sawed through the tough wire over the windows. Eventually I made it. A hole large enough for my body awaited me. Something held me back. I sat on the floor and stared at the hole, thinking hard.

What bothered me? I trust my instincts. I have to; they've kept me alive for a long time.

Then it hit me. I'd barely gotten to the edge of the clearing the first time when Faber appeared and turned on his magic wand. The gorilla had come after me even though Faber couldn't have seen me. After I'd dispatched the gorilla to its eternal banana republic in the sky, Faber had been waiting for me again, this time with a gimmicked room and the flight of tsetse flies.

I didn't think he'd prepared this special room sans doorknobs just for me. He hadn't had the time. This was a regular part of his paranoid world, a trap for the unwary, perhaps even a test room for the voracious flies. I envisioned a native tricked into this room while Faber watched to see what results his latest disease had on his unsuspecting victim. It wasn't a pretty picture, yet it was something I could see Faber enthusing over.

But he had known I had finished off the gorilla and then had lured me here. How had he known? I stared out the hole the wire mesh again, this time studying the area around the building more carefully.

"I'll be damned," I muttered to myself. On the porch behind a post stood a small home alarm unit like those sold by the big department stores in the U.S. Faber had outfitted his buildings with a motion sensor. I tripped it both times. I hadn't figured he would rely on mechanical or electronic gizmos; he was a biologist and, had he run true to form, would have been totally ignorant of such things.

I'd underestimated the man.

It wouldn't happen again.

Moving slower than molasses flowing uphill on a cold day, I edged through the screen. The motion sensors can be circumvented if movement is gradual enough. The designers didn't want a stray breeze moving a plant leaf to set off an alarm. Ever so carefully, I slipped through the wire mesh, onto the porch, and under the electronic umbrella put out by the alarm device.

Reaching up, taking pains to be sure my hand didn't enter the field, I switched off the machine.

"Now, Faber, we're down to a one-on-one."

I drew my Luger and went hunting.

Circling the building gave me no clues as to Faber's whereabouts. The sealed room—I was convinced now it was a test chamber for flying death—remained untouched. Dropping, I checked the dust outside the building for footprints. I found only small, indistinct indentations. But they led off into the forest. Following slowly, I made sure I didn't walk into another trap.

Instead, I found a small shed hidden among the trees. This had to be Faber's real laboratory. The expansive windows were equipped with fine-mesh screens but all the screens had been pulled up and away for better ventilation. I walked around the entire building, making sure that I hadn't missed anything. I was especially watchful for any more dime-store alarm systems.

The last one I'd come across had worked all too well.

I moved in for the kill.

The wooden porch creaked as my weight descended on it. I'm light on my feet but could do nothing about the protesting planks. I kept going until I came to the first window. Cautiously rising, I peered inside the lab.

The structure seemed larger inside than I'd've thought possible. It was one huge room lined with several rows of workbenches, all black-topped and stained with acids. An odor drifted forth from the lab that reminded me of the biology lab I'd taken in school. Formaldehyde. My nose wrinkled at the memories brought back by that pungent chemical smell.

A clinking of glassware caught my attention. I swiveled around and finally spotted Bron Faber. He worked with total concentration on some project, his back toward me. As he turned I got a good profile view. Wilhelmina came up but I held my fire. I saw what the man did and it chilled me to the bone.

In a test tube buzzed a tsetse fly. He stuck a syringe through the rubber stopper in the test tube. A bright, reflecting drop of a clear liquid dropped onto the fly. He shook the test tube to agitate the fly and soak it thoroughly in the liquid. I didn't need a Ph.D. in biology to know what was happening. That harmless-appearing clear liquid contained a bacteria or virus capable of wiping out a human life in a matter of seconds.

If I killed Faber now, he'd drop the syringe. It might or might not break. That didn't matter. A quick fire erased everything. But the test tube would break when it fell and a disease-carrying messenger of death would wing forth.

It was stupid of me to hesitate for even a second. What was one lousy tsetse fly compared to the infinite misery this man might cause? Still, the idea of that much death potential so close by had held me back for a second. No longer. I had been given a dangerous mission. It was time to complete it.

I waited for Faber to put down the test tube with the fly inside. My finger tensed. I fired just as Alleen yanked my hand up and away, ruining the shot. Glass tinkled inside the laboratory telling me that I'd missed Faber completely.

"Alleen, you fool!" I shouted. Shoving her out of my way, I kicked in the door and stood crouched, waiting for movement inside the room. If Faber so much as sneezed, I'd have him cold.

"Nick, don't hurt him. Please! I love him!"

"Stay back, Alleen," I snapped, my eyes never stopping their slow scan of the laboratory. "After what he's done to you, I'd think you'd want the son-of-a-bitch dead."

"You don't understand, do you, Carter?" came Faber's mocking voice. "She can't help herself. My first experiments were on insect control using pheromones. I adapted that to humans. My pheromones are absolutely irresistible to women." The diabolical laugh that followed told me to move out of the doorway. I silhouetted myself too much there. He might have a gun hidden away. Underestimating him again might prove fatal. I circled to the right, constantly on the alert.

"There's got to be more to it than that, Faber. You don't just smell good."

"It's sex-linked, Carter. Absolutely nonrational. Goes right to the most primitive instincts of humanity."

"With something like that, why bother with the tsetse fli

nd the disease? You have what all men dream about."

"Power. I want power. And you won't stop me, Carter.
No one will. I've issued an ultimatum to all the world leaders.
Of course, they didn't believe me. But they do now. I've
illed off ten of them. Told the press the exact time and
method, then killed those fools."

I had him pinpointed now. He crouched behind one of the
lack-topped work tables. Caution overrode my instinct to
eap up onto another table and start firing. If I missed him and
it any of the stoppered vials on the table, one of the horse-
nen of the Apocalypse—Faber's homemade plague—would
urely be released to gallop forth into the world.

I wanted to live to take the well-deserved R & R Hawk had
romised me.

"Bron, I love you so!" cried Alleen from the doorway.
"Please. Let me stay with you."

"He'll kill you, Alleen," I said. I hoped she would distract
im. If he exposed even one small portion of his body, I'd
ave him then. A bullet doesn't have much cross-section and
'm a good shot. Damn good.

"No, he won't. Please, Bron, let me . . ."

"Stay back!" he cried.

As he rose up I changed plans again. He held a large glass
eaker literally swarming with tsetse flies. Hundreds of them
ere inside. My eyes flashed to the large windows with the
aised screens. Those flies would be out the windows and
one in seconds. If they bred in the wild, it might be impossi-
le to stop the spread of a dozen different virulent diseases.

I dived straight for Faber, not even thinking of putting a
ullet through him. My hand closed on the wrist holding the
eaker. The angry buzzing of the flies inside told me what the
akes were.

"You won't win, Carter," he snarled, punching at me and
ying to get his hand free from the beaker. "They're infected
ith my own special disease. No antidote, no treatment—it
orks too fast."

I'd seen the results of his specially created disease. The

flesh rotted away from the body in minutes. Death wa
horrible. Hawk would have to order the entire area nuked t
keep the flies from spreading the disease worldwide.

Walvis Bay was a port for the west coast of Africa. On
pair of the tsetse flies could wipe out the entire continent i
they got aboard a freighter moving up the coast.

Or what if a ship bound for South America became in
fested? From there up through Central America and int
North America. I saw entire continents dying. And the sourc
of all that death and misery rubbed against my arm as I fough
to get it away from Faber.

He kneed me in the groin. I doubled up in pain, but ever
move I made came as the result of long training. I bent over
yes, but Hugo also slipped free from his sheath. My knif
drove upward into Faber's guts. The surprised look on hi
face told me he'd died almost instantly.

I regretted that he hadn't suffered like so many of hi
victims. Then I regretted killing him at all. The beake
containing the disease-carrying flies slipped from his hand.
grabbed for it but the blood spurting out of his belly made m
hands too slick. I felt like a prize receiver for a football tear
as I juggled the beaker.

As I closed my fingers on the neck of it, it popped up an
away from me. A loud crash sounded. The crash of doon
The flies buzzed angrily. They'd be out the windows i
seconds.

They would have been except for Alleen Kindt. She ha
watched my struggle with her lover. When the beaker brok
on the floor, she threw herself on top of it.

"God, Alleen," I said.

"The screens, Nick, drop the screens. Must, oh, m
stomach, the glass! M-must stop them from escaping. O
the flies!"

I knew the glass cut unmercifully into her body, but wh
she said was right. Running like a madman, I slammed ever
screen and then, when all were down, made the rounds aga

to securely lock them in place. Not one of those damned flies would leave here.

"Done, Alleen. I . . ."

My throat constricted at the sight. Bron Faber had nurtured the perfect disease. Quick acting, it had already claimed Alleen in the most gruesome manner possible. She lay half-turned on the floor, clutching at the beaker cutting into her stomach. Her once beautiful features had twisted in unbearable pain. She hadn't been more than twenty-one. She now looked a hundred. Her skin wrinkled and fell from her bones. There wasn't any blood. Somehow, the fast-acting disease had sucked up her life's juices. I watched in mute horror as she aged another hundred years in seconds. Alleen had turned into a mummy.

The pain and terror she'd felt in those last seconds of life remained on her face, etched there forever.

"Alleen," I said, my throat dry and voice choked. I saw the tsetse flies working their way out from under her body. Shock wore off and I sprang into action. I found a metal tin of methyl alcohol. I poured it over her and lit the volatile liquid from a nearby Bunsen burner. The bright blue flames licked at her once-gorgeous body.

The flies were caught in the intense flame and cremated. I swatted a few escaping in other directions. For over an hour I patrolled that laboratory, trying not to look at the ravaged corpse on the floor, as I hunted down every possible fly. Only when I was positive that every single one of the airborne killers had perished did I search the lab.

I found Faber's notebooks. I carefully ripped the pages out and crumpled them. Then I found more alcohol and doused the papers. A last bit of bright, cleansing flame from the Bunsen burner ignited the notes, the floor, and the benches.

I left then and stood outside watching, until only charred supports remained of the building. Even then, I waited and listened, dreading the sound of the normal African insects buzzing around my head, praying that I wouldn't hear a tsetse fly.

Only when I assured myself that I'd eliminated every single fly did I leave. It was a long drive back to Walvis Bay.

"It is a shame, N3, that you couldn't have found Faber's notebooks," said Hawk. "They might have given us great insight into prevention of disease."

"He only caused it," I said glumly. I sat across from Hawk, his immense desk between us. After getting back to Walvis Bay, I'd radioed the States, told Hawk all that had happened—with a few major changes—and then waited for pickup. That night a Sea Stallion helicopter landed, took me out to a carrier in the Atlantic, and from there I was flown into Washington, D.C. I'd been back less than three hours.

"Being able to cause a disease is an important step in finding ways to prevent and cure them, N3. You know that." He studied me with those piercing, cold eyes of his. "It's a terrible weapon, isn't it?" he said more softly.

"You had to see it for yourself to believe it, sir," I said. In my mind I still pictured Alleen aging so quickly, eaten alive by the voracious disease spawned by Faber.

"And it wouldn't do to let just anyone have this power. We might all turn into Bron Fabers. Isn't that what you're thinking, Nick?"

"What?" The use of my first name surprised me. During debriefings, Hawk is usually all business. "Yes, you're right."

"Well, that's *not* right. The United States would never use such a weapon. But we have to have the weapon, nonetheless. Sticking our heads in the sand won't stop others from developing biowarfare weapons even more dangerous."

"It might."

"It won't. Stop sounding like an idiot, Nick. You're upset right now over this woman's death. You gave a very graphic description. But think on this. If we'd had Faber's knowledge of diseases, he would have been powerless against anyone. If we could cure as easily as he infected, we could have laughed at him."

"Would we have been so free with the antidote?" I asked. "To a country whose policies we don't fully support?"

"I can't answer that, Nick, in any way that will satisfy you at this moment. Ugly things happen in the world. The U.S. is usually left with the unenviable task of tidying them up. We don't cause too many of those ugly things, but we have to deal with them."

"Garbageman to the world." I snorted and shook my head sadly.

"Call it what you will. You did a good job. The world owes you a debt of gratitude—and no one outside this office will ever know." He paused for a moment, then added, "Isn't the knowledge of a job well done, a *necessary* job well done, reward enough?"

He knew that wasn't what ate away at me.

"I could have saved her. I shouldn't have let her come with me. Not that last time."

"She had valuable information, N3. By your own standards, she died as good a death as anyone could hope for. She saved countless lives by sacrificing her own. She stopped a plague for which there might not have been a quick cure. She died; your burden is continuing to live."

I thought about what Hawk said. He was right, of course. That's what I envy about him. Winning an argument is hard because he usually comes out on top. Alleen had given her life for millions, millions who would never know that she had even lived, much less saved them from awful death. She had been honest and decent and, when it counted most, brave.

And there hadn't been anything I could have done to stop her from accompanying me. She had a single-minded determination to find Faber. Even if I'd left her in Walvis Bay, she'd have somehow found him. It might even be for the best, this way. Faber's genetic engineering had twisted her round. Now she was free of his influence—forever.

"Go on your vacation, Nick. You've earned it."

I stood and went to the door.

"Nick?" he called.

"Sir?"

"Any idea where you're going to take that R & R?"

"Somewhere without flies," I said.

But Hawk wasn't listening. He already turned to the next crisis brewing. I left, aching in body and spirit, but finally sure that things had returned to normal.

DON'T MISS THE NEXT NEW
NICK CARTER SPY THRILLER

THE CHRISTMAS KILL

On the seventh punch to the right kidney, I felt consciousness leaving for good.

I opened my eyes, saw someone move past the shade in the lighted office, saw hands go up in some kind of angry gesture, then closed my eyes and dropped off the edge of the earth.

Later, but not much later, I felt movement and then heard the high-pitched whine of a small engine. I was in a car. In the trunk. I could feel the spare tire against my spine.

I conked out again.

The next time I awoke, light was streaming through a window. It looked like a window and yet it wasn't a window. On closer examination by my swollen, aching eyes, I saw that it was a hole in the wall. A jagged hole.

I groaned and moved my head. The movement sent pain up

and down my body, reminding my brain that pain had been there all along.

All around me on a wooden floor were chunks of debris, most of it charred, as though a furious fire or intense heat had at one time been in or close to this building.

I gazed at the ceiling. Wooden timbers showed through broken plaster. I could see into a room above, and a room above that. Beyond at least three floors was a roof. There were jagged holes in that roof, letting in light from the sky.

My first thought was that I was in a hotel and had miraculously survived a tremendous explosion. It was like being left behind in a part of hell that had been abandoned by others as an intolerable place to exist.

There was no furniture in the room. It had been consumed in the fire or blown through the walls and ceiling by the explosion.

Suddenly, I knew where I was.

The old ruins at one end of Peace Park.

The building that had been gutted by the atomic bomb blast of more than thirty-five years ago, and left as a memorial to that holocaust.

The building that was off-limits to visitors. No one ever came inside this building. In time, it would tumble into a pile of rubble all on its own.

And I knew then that the black-hooded men had left me alive so that I could suffer and die in this empty, abandoned, unvisited building.

Repayment, retribution, a symbolic eye-for-an-eye gesture.

One more victim of the A-bomb blast that took seventy-five thousand lives in the twinkling of an eye, and left tens of thousands more to die of burns and radiation.

And that victim was to be me, Nick Carter, N3, Killmaster for AXE. That victim was to be the phony toy salesman named Peter Holmes.

Not, by God, if I could help it.

I moved my head again, trying to see through the gaping hole to my right.

Pain rattled up and down my body. My kidneys came alive with complaint. Agonizing complaint.

Again and again, I tried to move various parts of my body. Movement of my head set off all sorts of pains. The same thing happened when I tried to move my hands and legs. Jesus, I couldn't even swivel my eyeballs without setting off rockets of agony damned near everywhere in my body.

I stopped trying to move. Give it time, my mind said. In time, maybe only an hour or so, I'll get the hell out of here and find help.

The hunger pangs found their way through all that pain. Thirst was rampant. Christ, had I lost so much blood that I was literally dying of hunger and dehydration?

No. I'd lost only a little blood, through my nose. There were no open wounds that a mental check of my body could detect.

The deep hunger and parching thirst came from one thing.

Time.

I had apparently been in this building for some time. Perhaps days. The light of the sky was not merely the dawn of the day after my visit to the factory and my encounter with those seven men in black hoods.

It was the middle of the second, third, fourth, or fifth day.

No. The human body can go without water no more than seventy-two hours. Some anxious sense deep inside me told me that I had used up most, if not all, of those seventy-two hours by being totally unconscious.

I tried to scream, to attract attention. Peace Park was always full of visitors. Someone would hear, call the police. It was better to rest in a Japanese jail as a fugitive from immigration—having entered the country with a false passport—than to die of thirst in this ruin from the first A-bomb blast.

Nothing but pain came from my throat. My lips, swollen

and bloody from the beating and from thirst, barely parted for sound that would not come.

I tried to raise myself again, with the same agonizing results. I passed out several times from sheer pain.

Panic threatened to take control.

Once or twice I slept and dreamed how pleasant it would be to simply die and escape all this pain. A sense of euphoria overcame me and I knew that I was in danger.

Wishing to die is the final step before death itself.

But the euphoria was strong, overcoming my sense of danger.

I lay still, no longer fighting, no longer trying to move, welcoming death, wishing it would hurry.

—From THE CHRISTMAS KILL
A New Nick Carter Spy Thriller
From Ace Charter in January